MW01202153

Donnell's Sultry Treat

Seven Giants Series: Book Four

MzSassytheAuthor

Donnell's Sultry Treat

Copyright © 2021 by MzSassytheAuthor.

All rights reserved. Printed in the United States of America. No part of this book may be used or reproduced in any manner whatsoever without written permission except in the case of brief quotations embodied in critical articles or reviews.

This book is a work of fiction. Names, characters, businesses, organizations, places, events, and incidents either are the product of the author's imagination or are used fictitiously. Any resemblance to actual persons, living or dead, events, or locales is entirely coincidental.

Contact the Author:
mzsassytheauthor@gmail.com
Instagram: mzsassytheauthor
Facebook.com/mzsassytheauthor
Twitter: mzsassytheauth1
Facebook Bookclub: Sassy Savvy Stories
TikTok: mzsassytheauthor

Book and Cover design by:
Amethyst Phoenix Press

First Edition: November 2021
ISBN: 9781736972243

Chapter One

The neighborhood was quiet for an October afternoon in Houston. Donnell Mason parked his car in front of his friend Darwin's townhouse and cut his engine. He reached for the box of goodies in his passenger seat and exited his vehicle. Walking around his car then heading up the walkway, he rang the doorbell as he reached the porch.

"Donnie, I'm so glad you could make it." Kelsey exclaimed. Kelsey was Darwin's girlfriend and the mother of their five-year-old daughter Kaley.

"Come on in." she took a step back to allow him entry into their home. Once inside, she reached up to greet him with a hug, which he gladly accepted.

"Happy Birthday!" Donnell said while embracing her.

"Thank you. Are those for me?" She asked, releasing him and noticing the box in his hand."

"I believe so." He said, almost handing her the box.

"Oh, no you don't." They both heard Darwin say, quickly approaching. He took the box before Donnell had the chance to give it to Kelsey.

"Darwin, what are you hiding?" Kelsey asked.

"Not hiding, just surprising." Darwin replied.

"I smell lemon." she said excitedly. Darwin shook his head.

"Later." he warned, clutching the box tighter. He greeted Donnell and led him through his townhouse to the backyard. A few tables were set up with decorations in yellow. Darwin introduced him to other party-goers, and Donnell greeted them.

"What took you so long?" His cousin Dillon asked.

"Standard Houston traffic." He answered.

"Did you know you could decorate so many things in yellow? I'm expecting Big Bird to jump out anytime now." he had a point. Everything was decorated in yellow, from the tablecloth to the cutlery, even the grill had a yellow stripe. Donnell frowned, hoping that wouldn't attract any bees.

"Is Dexter coming today?" Donnell asked Dillon. Dillon told him he should arrive shortly with another one of their friends, Damien. He nodded, knowing two of their friends Dominic and Dustin, could not make it. There were seven of them in total. Dillon, Dexter, Dustin, Dominic,

Darwin, Damien, and himself. Earning them the nickname the 'Seven Giants' in college. That had been his idea while pledging. The fraternity wanted to call them the seven dwarfs as part of their theme, but at 6'7", he would never consider himself a dwarf. He grabbed a bottle of water while Kelsey's friend Mandy took over DJ duties. The backdoor opened, and Darwin and Kelsey's daughter, Kaley, walked out. She was wearing a yellow dress, or more so, a ball gown. She ran over to her father, who gladly picked her up and signed; what Donnell assumed was that she looked pretty. Kaley did not speak, but she was a brilliant little girl. Kaley attended the Knight Foundation, a school started by Darwin's late mother, Susan Knight, for children with special needs struggling with communication skills. A few moments later, Darwin's father arrived, Bishop Joshua Knight. He made his rounds, speaking to those in attendance before making his way over to where Donnell and Dillon stood.

"It's good to see the both of you." he said, extending his hand. Dillon took it first and shook it in greeting.

"It's nice to see you again also, sir." Donnell said, accepting his hand after Dillon. Donnell remembered meeting Bishop Knight a couple of times while they were in college. Donnell's mother wasn't as traditional in attending church on Sunday as Dillon's mom had, but Donnell liked that Bishop Knight seemed like an ordinary man while on campus. He made sure to say a prayer for them before he left, and Donnell never felt as though the bible was being thrown at them or that Bishop Knight was condemning them. Although Donnell was pretty sure he considered it, with Damien and Dexter, especially during their college days. Dexter toned down his interaction with women shortly after college. Damien only recently seemed to slow down. As if his thoughts could conjure them up, Damien and Dexter walked through the backdoor, followed by Shannon, Dominic's cousin, and Kelsey. They made their rounds of greetings before Dexter, Damien, and Shannon headed over to where they stood, greeting Bishop Knight in passing.

"Who knew you could decorate so much in yellow?" Dexter grunted.

"Well, she is an interior designer." Shannon chimed in.

"You guys know what Darwin has planned, right?" Damien asked. Each of them looked at him in confusion.

"Well, it wasn't a surprise party." Dillon answered. Damien looked at each of them then walked back over to Darwin. Each of them watched the exchange in words before Damien threw his head back and laughed while clapping Darwin on the back.

"Do you have any idea what that was about?" Dexter asked.

"No, but Darwin is messing with Damien. Most likely, it is about Kelsey." Donnell said.

"Do you think she still has that calendar pin-up of Damien?" Dillon joked. Dexter frowned, causing Donnell, Shannon, and Dillon to laugh.

"You're joking, right?" Dexter questioned.

"Where have you been that you missed that detail?" Shannon asked.

"I do have a business to run." Dexter stated flatly. Dexter owned a fitness empire called 'Dex-It'.

"Still, you should know how much hell Damien has been giving Darwin over it." Dillon added.

"Seems like Darwin is getting him back." Shannon stated, enjoying the thought a little more than the rest of them. Donnell shook his head. The interaction with his friends was crazy, but he wouldn't have it any other way.

"Where are Dominic and Dustin?" Dexter asked, as if finally realizing they were missing.

"Dominic is in Boston with Ashiree. They are house hunting." Shannon said.

"House hunting? Are they moving to Boston?" Dillon asked.

"No, just getting a second home there." Shannon responded. Donnell noticed the deflate in her voice. He wondered how well she was adjusting to the new changes in her cousin's life. For years, it had just been the two of them. Dominic and Shannon were extremely close after losing their parents in a plane crash almost twenty-five years ago. More like brother and sister than mere cousins. Dominic's marriage to Ashiree last year had been a shock to all of them, considering they hadn't known each other long. However, Donnell witnessed his friend falling head over heels for his wife. He saw it as a positive change from the tragic loss of their grandfather, Donald Blake, only a couple of months prior. Donald Blake had been a pillar of power and influence in Houston, most of the country, and various industries.

"What about Dustin?" Dexter asked again, breaking Donnell's thoughts.

"He's probably chained to a bed." Dillon answered nonchalantly, then further explained as the three of them looked at him in confusion. "I talked to him a couple of days ago. Nadia wants a baby, or Tricia...what the heck are we supposed to call her?" Dillon asked earnestly. Donnell chuckled. The situation between Dustin and his wife was slightly confusing. Nadia Bolton, also known as Tricia Hanson, was married to their friend Dustin. Dustin met

Nadia at Ashiree's baby shower a few months back. They all soon discovered that Nadia had lost her memory twelve years ago, around the same time a girl named Tricia Hanson supposedly died. Donnell rubbed a hand down his face remembering working on the case. As an independent intel operative for the CIA, he could research or dig into any case, file, or document with a digital print. Nadia's case was old and stemmed from a scandal where five women were illegally kidnapping women's babies in correctional facilities. Illegal adoptions were set up for a very nice sum of money. Nadia, or rather Tricia's birth, had been the start of how they could pull it off.

"I believe she agreed to file her name as Tricia Nadia Shaw." Donnell answered, still helping sort a few things out.

Little Kaley approached them with Damien following, holding a tray of lemon treats. She smiled brightly, serving each of them a treat with a yellow napkin.

"Thank you, Kaley." Donnell heard Shannon say sweetly and pinched the little girl's cheek. Giggling, Kaley led Damien over to a few others.

"Oh, I have got to get a picture of this." Dillon said, pulling out his phone.

"I want a copy." Dexter said as Dillon took several pictures of Damien being led around holding a tray of sweets for Kaley to hand out.

"If you two think for one second, those pictures are going to embarrass him, don't waste your time. Women go crazy over a man helping a kid." Shannon said. Donnell watched the excitement leave Dillon's eyes as he put his phone up. Chuckling slightly, he picked up the treat, took a bite, and nearly moaned out loud. The moment the cream-filled treat hit his tongue, a burst of flavor exploded in his mouth. He took another bite without missing a beat, convinced he hadn't experienced what he thought, and was pleasantly surprised by the same reaction.

"What is this?" he heard Dillon ask, eating his treat with the same surprised reaction Donnell had.

"I think it's some kind of tart." Shannon asked, also taking another bite.

"It can't be that good." Dexter stated, still holding his treat in his hand.

"Try it." Donnell encouraged, finishing his treat and practically licking his fingers.

"Where did Darwin get these?" Dillon asked, finishing his treat as well.

"A new bakery off I-45. I picked them up before I came here." Donnell was stretching his neck to glance over to the dessert table to see if there were more.

"I stand corrected. This is good. I am not normally

into sweets. I'll probably have to plan an extra workout to burn it off." Dexter said.

"I think you can handle one, Dex." Dillon replied. Donnell's eyes finally landed on a few more treats on the table, and he excused himself to get another one. Reaching the table, he saw a few other assorted goodies; none of them looked the same. Donnell unashamedly grabbed three and walked back over to the group.

"You really do have a sweet tooth." Shannon teased. Donnell didn't pay her any attention. While he'd walked over to the dessert table, Damien made his way back over to them. Donnell took another bite, and the same burst of flavors hit his mouth yet again. This time, he moaned out loud.

"Dude, you seriously need to get laid." Dillon stated. Damien chuckled, but Donnell ignored him. Swirls of sweetness invaded his mouth as he finished yet another treat. Each one reminded him of the baker he'd only seen for a moment while picking the goodies up. Chocolate eyes. That's what he remembered: her chocolate eyes, her full figure under her apron, her smile while she talked to other customers.

"Donnie, you might want to turn around." he heard Shannon whisper. He did as she suggested while bringing another treat to his lips and stopped at the scene across from them. Darwin was down on one knee, with Kaley at his side, proposing to Kelsey. She instantly said yes before Darwin could finish whatever speech he had prepared. The congradulations of everyone watching and cheering halted Donnell's assault on the last dessert he held. He placed it on the small table close to where they were standing as each of them walked over to congratulate the newly engaged couple.

"And then there were four." Donnell heard Dexter grunt afterward. Shannon rolled her eyes at Dexter. Dillon and Damien began to discuss which of them would be next to take the plunge, but Donnell focused on his last treat. Not even attempting to be polite while he devoured the whole thing, closing his eyes, allowing all the delectable flavors to saturate his mouth. The only thought that entered Donnell's mind after he'd swallowed the last morsel is he would see the new baker again, and soon.

Brandy Pearce opened the back door to her bakery and walked in. Closing the door behind her and locking it, she hung her purse on the hook in the back hallway and turned on the lights. She found her row of aprons and lightly tapped her finger to her lips.

"Which one are we wearing today?" she thought

aloud. She picked the black and yellow striped one, placed it over her head, and tied it around her waist. It made her midsection look like a giant bumblebee. Smiling at her choice, she knew it was perfect for the cinnamon honey delights she would batch up this morning. Brandy instructed Alexa to play her playlist and began moving around her kitchen, grabbing her ingredients, turning on her mixers and oven. She stirred and kneaded the dough to the sound of the music playing. Soon the aroma of the bakery was filled with all the different honey accented donuts, tarts, and pastries. Tray in hand, she left her kitchen to head to the front dining area. It wasn't a large space, but enough for a display case and a small counter for her cash register, a few small tables and chairs lined against the window, and even a kiddie table with a few coloring books and crayons. She opened the back of the display case and began placing and arranging the items from her tray. The coffee and espresso machine was turned on next before she headed back into the kitchen for the next round of treats. She heard the charm ring from the back door and wiped her hands on a towel to answer it.

"Good Morning!" Staci greeted Brandy as she opened the door. It was close to five-thirty in the morning, and the bakery would open soon. Her best friend, Staci, graciously helped her the last two weeks in getting the bakery started. Staci worked the afternoon shift at a retirement home and spent her mornings helping Brandy with the bakery.

"Good Morning to you." Brandy greeted, stepping back to allow Staci entrance.

"It smells good in here. I'm telling you, my nose thanks you, but my waistline is not too happy with you." They shared a laugh. Staci had been taking home the treats not sold to her family.

"I'm sure the kids appreciate it."

"Not as much as me. Neil's mom is in town, and I have been allowing the kids extra treats before heading off to work."

"You are so wrong, Staci."

"That woman drives me nuts. I'm still not happy with her inviting Neil's ex-girlfriend to our wedding as her plus one." Staci complained, hanging her purse and sweater up. Brandy laughed as Staci grabbed her signature pink and white apron and continued her verbal assault against her mother-in-law. Eventually, the conversation steered toward the kids and, of course, the ladies and gentlemen at the retirement home.

"I'm telling you, Brandy, those old ladies are some freaks. I caught Ms. Alma grabbing Mr. Charles by the butt as he walked down the hall." Brandy snickered.

"They're old, not dead, Staci. I'm sure they still have...needs."

"Oh, that just put a bad taste in my mouth. You should give me a tart to fix it." Staci suggested. Brandy laughed.

"You were just waiting for an opening. But actually, I have something new that I'd love for you to try." Brandy reached for one of the batter bowls she was mixing. "Taste this." She said, handing Staci a taster stick with the new batter.

"Mmmm, oh my goodness. That's so good."

"Do you really like it?"

"Yes, oh yeah." Staci nodded, grabbing another taste stick and trying to get some more.

"I can't decide if I want to try it as a glaze or a filling." Brandy stated.

"Either works for me, but that's a lot of filling for donuts."

"True, but I was thinking of a surprise filling in one of the tarts."

"That will work. A lot of the customers love the surprise fillings." Staci confirmed. One of Brandy's specialties was that she laced her treats with hidden flavors. It was her signature mark. Brandy spent a few minutes discussing her ideas with Staci before the alarm went off, indicating it was time to open the bakery. She and Staci quickly moved to the main dining area. Staci double-checked everything with the coffee machine and opened the front door. A few customers were waiting outside, which was always a good sign. Greeting them and taking their orders, the morning rush seemed to come and go.

"I'm going to make a quick run to the bathroom while we have a break." Staci announced. Brandy nodded and headed back to the kitchen to grab another tray of treats when the bell over the front door chimed. Deciding to hurry, Brandy quickly grabbed the tray and headed back out to the front. A very tall man was in her bakery.

"Good Morning. Give me just a second." She said, balancing the tray to open the display case.

"Take your time." The tall gentleman said, and Brandy almost lost her grip on the tray hearing his deep, husky voice. She managed to get the tray into the case without dropping it. Shaking off the effects of the man's voice, she stood and put on her best customer service smile.

"Welcome to Branded Flavors. What can I get for you?" She watched a slow smile appear on his face before he spoke.

"What do you recommend?" he asked.

"Is this your first time here?" she replied, wondering why her body was warming under his gaze.

"Yes and no. I was here to pick up an order a few days ago for a friend. The assortment of lemon-themed treats was surprisingly amazing. I didn't realize I liked lemon until then." Brandy smiled, remembering the Knight order. She found it a little strange when she saw the 'all things lemon' order. Her store had not officially opened when the order was placed. She had been doing small catering events with desserts for family and friends for the last couple of years. Mainly special occasions like birthday parties, bachelorette parties, engagement parties, and some weddings. The increasing demand for her treats was a deciding factor in her finally taking the plunge and opening her own bakery. It allowed her to have much better use of space than her small bedroom apartment.

"I remember that order. It was my first time using that much lemon. Did your friend enjoy them?" She inquired. She'd sent a follow-up email asking for a customer review and had not received a response yet. Brandy found it also strange that she did not recall seeing him. There were so many customers on the day of her Grand Opening. How had she missed him?

"I think he did. But I'm sure they were

overshadowed by the diamond ring he gave to his now fiancé."

"Oh, that's amazing. Congratulations to them." Brandy said, watching as he looked over into the display case.

"So, technically, I'm still a newbie. What do you recommend?"

"Well, today's theme is all things honey." She announced. He stood back to his full height, and his eyes slowly raked over her full-figured body.

"That explains the bee apron." He said with a wink. Brandy was sure if she could blush, her cheeks would be bright red. The temperature in her body rose a little.

"Yes." she answered, catching her breath and showing the items in the display case. She watched as he placed his hand under his chin and rubbed slowly in thought. Immediately taking notice of his hand, Brandy swallowed hard. As a baker, she used her hands a lot. While working with other culinary artists, Brandy always noticed their hands. The slow movement of his hand rubbing his chin kept her in a daze. His fingers were long, and she could see the muscled veins in his hands, not too big or small, but perfect.

"I guess I'll have to try them all." She blinked, realizing he'd been talking while trying to decide. She needed to get it together.

"Are you sure?"

"Yes, I'd hate to miss the opportunity to taste them." She quickly shifted to grab a platter box and tongs. Every word out of his mouth wreaked havoc on her senses, especially the one that allowed her to function correctly. She rang up his order and offered coffee. He declined, thanked her, and left. Brandy watched him through the front window as he got into his car and pulled away.

"Sorry I took so long, but I had to explain to my mother-in-law where the extra bed linens were. Little Neil had an accident last night." Staci said, coming to stand beside Brandy.

"Um, Hm." Brandy managed to say, leaning on the counter, still staring out the window.

"What in the world is going on with you, Brandy? Brandy?" she blinked, finally standing and looking over at Staci.

"I'm sorry. What were you talking about?"

"Forget what I was talking about," Staci said, looking toward the window and slightly frowned when she saw nothing that would cause Brandy to stare. "What were you looking at? Was there an altercation in the parking lot?" Staci asked.

"No, I got lost in my thoughts." Brandy answered

and turned to straighten up a few things on the counter.

"Must have been some amazing thoughts." Staci answered and began helping to clean. Brandy smiled to herself. Yes, some amazing thoughts indeed.

Chapter Two

"**I swear** I think you're obsessed." Dillon teased Donnell. Donnell ignored him as they all gathered in the sitting area of Blake Manor. Every Thursday night, his friend Dominic's wife, Ashiree, hosted dinner at their home. He and his friends, along with Dominic's cousin Shannon, attempted to attend as much as possible. After Ashiree was kidnapped and rescued last year, she began inviting them over. Ashiree grew up in the foster system and kept to herself and her best friend Chelsea, who lived in Boston. Donnell knew this was Ashiree's way of embracing her new life with Dominic and creating some sense of normalcy. Dominic Blake was born into wealth. His late grandfather, Donald Blake, started Blake Inc. by selling simple electronics, but truly made his fortune investing in the cable's expansion industry. Blake Inc, now known as Blake Enterprises, was a billion-dollar corporation involved in other sectors, including finance, communications, then expanded into pharmaceutical markets, leading Dominic to reconnect with Ashiree.

"What has Donnie become obsessed with?" Dominic asked, sitting beside his wife with his six-month-old son on his lap.

"Some new bakery on the southeast side." Dillon answered. Dillon owned a sports bar named Quills. Their grandfather started it during a time when most blacks didn't own businesses. However, his grandfather overcame that obstacle after serving in the war. Many of his patrons were his army buddies, both black and white. After his grandfather passed away, Donnell's father had taken over and kept the bar going for nearly twenty years. Not too long after he and Dillon graduated college, his father was involved in a car accident that hindered his walking ability, confining him to a wheelchair. Both he and Dillon were working for MIT, attempting to make a name for themselves. They were well on their way, talked about by many as the Mason Duo. Donnell was proud to work alongside his cousin. Outside of Dillon's playful attitude, he was brilliant. Smarter than Donnell in many ways, but Dillon had a heart and a way with people that Donnell didn't possess. When his father was in the hospital, Dillon stepped up and helped run Quills. Donnell helped for a few weekends, not wanting to lose their grandfather's most valued possession but when the doctor confirmed that his father would never walk again, talks of shutting the sports bar down were amongst their family. Dillon walked away from MIT without batting an eye. His father was furious with him, as he had not been a fan of keeping the bar. Dillon hadn't budged, and Donnell's father signed Quills over to Dillon. It was going on strong almost seven years since the accident, and Dillon couldn't be happier, even with the constant ridicule from his father.

"How many times have you been there?" Ashiree asked.

"Only a handful." Donnell answered modestly. He'd visited every day that week, but he did not need everyone to know. It was more than the treats that drew him to the bakery.

"Wait, is that the place where you picked up the lemon tarts?" Kelsey asked.

"Yes." Donnell answered.

"Oh my goodness, they were so good when I had them at my birthday party." Kelsey exclaimed.

"The birthday party that someone decided to make a surprise proposal at?" Ashiree asked, her dry sarcasm directed at Darwin.

"I'm not sure how many times I can apologize for that, Ashiree. It was truly last minute." Darwin tried to explain. A few chuckles were heard in the room as Ashiree was a little upset that she had missed Darwin's proposal to

Kelsey. Ashiree and Kelsey formed a nice friendship over the last few months.

"Don't worry, and you can help me plan the wedding." Kelsey suggested.

"Oh, you know I am not good at that. How about I help you find a wedding planner?" Ashiree offered.

"That works, but who helped you plan your wedding?" Kelsey asked.

"Shannon." Ashiree replied.

"And I am not volunteering." Shannon quickly replied, taking a sip from her martini glass.

"Oh, come on, Shannon, you did an excellent job." Ashiree praised.

"That was a special circumstance, and there was no way I was leaving it up to Dominic."

"Hey, I did a pretty good job setting things up." Dominic interjected.

"You forgot to order the cake and pick up the rings." Shannon countered.

"I asked Damien to pick up the rings." Dominic explained. Damien Storm was the son of former baseball player Dante Storm and lingerie empire mogul Danica Storm. Also born into wealth, but he held a larger scale of celebrity status than Dominic. Following in his father's footsteps, Damien also became a baseball player, almost beating each of his father's records.

"That just proves my point." Shannon said. Four sets of eyes looked at Damien.

"What?" Damien began. "I thought Dominic was joking or possibly drunk. "Who calls out of the blue asking someone to pick up wedding rings? He hadn't even said he was getting married." Damien finished. Kelsey chuckled, Shannon rolled her eyes, and Ashiree shook her head.

"We'll get someone to help us?" Ashiree confirmed.

"Yes, and we should definitely get that bakery to cater the desserts." Kelsey said.

"What is the name of the bakery?" Dominic asked.

"Branded Flavors, I think?" Darwin answered, looking at Donnell for confirmation.

"Yes, the owner's name is Brandy." Donnell confirmed.

"Oh, that's cute." Kelsey added.

"Well, I might consider investing in this, Branded Flavors." Dominic said, emphasizing the name while looking at Ashiree.

"You're thinking about getting into the food industry now?" Dillon asked.

"If this bakery is as good as it seems and keeps Donnie from asking my wife to bake for him, I'll ensure the place never closes." Dominic stated. Donnell belted out a laugh, and Ashiree playfully swatted at Dominic. It wasn't a secret that Dominic and Ashiree were playing, teasing one another. Ashiree loved to bake as a pastime, and Donnell could admit she was pretty good. But he'd played Devil's advocate a few months back, allowing Ashiree to bribe him with some baked goodies in exchange for him changing the door code to the two-story colonial that sat behind Blake Manor. It was built by Dominic's father and had been Dominic's childhood home before his parents died. Dominic had given it to Ashiree. She felt more comfortable in the colonial than at the Manor. Dominic suggested Ashiree quit her job after fainting while pregnant, which added to his worry for her after being kidnapped last year. It was in all good fun that Donnell had helped Ashiree with her task that day. Even with Dominic appearing jealous of the slight bond between him and Ashiree, he knew his friend was only joking. The conversation continued as dinner was called, and everyone adjourned to the dining room together.

"**I can't** believe you told him I was single." Brandy ranted to Staci.

"Come on, Brandy. The guy is here practically every

day. I think it is safe to say he is interested in more than just the goodies in the display case." Staci answered. Brandy chose to ignore her and stirred the mix in the bowl a little more intensely than needed. She could use her mixture but, right now, she needed something to put her frustration on. Staci was right. The customer, Donnell was his name, had been in her bakery every morning around ten, almost like clockwork. They lightly flirted, but Staci went too far when Brandy was by-passing some of Donnell's questions. He now knew she attended culinary school, thanks to Staci. Found out she was better at baking than cooking, thanks to Staci. Her favorite color was blue, she loved female R & B artists like Monica, Brandy, and Alicia Keys, and her all-time favorite sitcom was Moesha. Again, all thanks to Staci.

"I'm not interested, Staci." Brandy lied.

"Oh, please. You lose your ability to speak when he's around." Staci said.

"I do not." Brandy denied.

"You do too." Staci countered. She did, but it was hard not to. At 31, one would think Brandy would have a better grip on herself around the opposite sex. In most cases, she did, but not now. If Brandy were completely honest with herself, she looked forward to seeing him. Not that she would ever tell Staci. If Brandy confessed one ounce of interest in Donnell, Staci would start planning her wedding. She almost groaned out loud. That was never happening. Brandy decided long ago that marriage was not something she ever wanted. Clearly, the vows and oaths said by couples claiming they were in love before God and witnesses was all an act. No one knew they if could commit themselves to one person for the rest of their lives. Her parents taught her that. Or at least her father had. She didn't want to think about her father or what she believed was the greatest betrayal a man could make. It wasn't enough for her father to step out on her mother; he'd hidden an entire family for years. She had grown up a daddy's girl, thinking her father could do no wrong. She felt her parents' marriage was so perfect, her life was so perfect, but it had all been a lie and came crashing down before her eyes.

At fourteen years old, what was supposed to be a day of family time and a trip with her father turned out to be the worst day of her life. Well, it was probably worse for her mother, but it had been just as shocking to her. They were all together at the Natural Museum of Science. An eighth-grade graduation trip or outing she would never forget. It was a Thursday afternoon when the museum had free entry and practically every intermediate school in the Houston area was visiting. They were just leaving the dinosaur exhibit as her dad made a corny joke about the short arms of a tyrannosaurus Rex when she heard a girl call out 'dad'. With so many other students and kids around, Brandy had thought nothing of it.

There were parents, teachers, and other chaperones all around. The thought never crossed her mind the girl was calling out to her dad. She'd kept walking only to notice her mother stiffened beside her, and her dad stopped entirely. The girl called out to her dad again, and Brandy finally turned to see her. The first thing she noticed was her small-shaped figure and short height. She'd looked up at her mother, wearing an expression that Brandy could not make out. Her dad had looked over at them and then slowly turned to the girl and spoke to her. She asked her mother what was going on. Why was this girl calling for her daddy? Her mother never answered her. Her father looked sad or regretful as he found one chaperone to take her back to the other student she came with. Brandy was confused and bombarded her father with questions as they immediately left. She only stopped at the request of her mother. Her father never answered her questions. The tension between her parents on the car ride home could be cut with a knife and lasted for days. During an argument she overheard while listening in the hall closest to her parent's bedroom, she learned the girl at the museum was her sister. She had a sister, and one very close in age, to her own. Her father had been unfaithful and in the worst way. His consistent travel schedule was not because of his work but his need to be present with his other family.

Her parents' marriage ended soon after. Her mother was embarrassed, and Brandy was furious with her father for his betrayal. She learned her sister's name was Raven, a sister that even to this day she refused to meet.

"I think you should go out with him." Staci said, interrupting her thoughts. She blinked, refocusing on the conversation they had been having. Oh, the almost seven-foot Adonis that walked into her bakery looking to taste all her treats. She almost laughed to herself at her choice of words.

"That would require him actually asking me out." Brandy replied casually as she grabbed a bowl of gelatin from the frig.

"Would you go with him if he asked?" Staci questioned. Brandy put the bowl on the counter and grabbed a spoon before looking at her friend. Would she go out with him? Probably, but she didn't want to tell Staci that.

"I would consider it." she said, downplaying her attraction. Although, she was pretty sure Staci wasn't buying it.

"I'm sure you would. I could even..." Staci began.

"No." Brandy interrupted firmly. "No more interference from you. If he is interested, he will need to ask me himself. You got that?"

"My, my, testy, testy, aren't we?" Staci said, throwing her hands up in mock surrender. "I will back off," she continued to say as she grabbed some creamer and began to head out of the kitchen and into the dining area. "For now." she added with a wink before leaving the kitchen. Brandy shook her head at her silly friend. She knew Staci wanted her to be overly besotted in love as she was. Experiencing her own happily ever after as Staci saw it. The problem was, Brandy didn't believe in happily ever after.

Before heading to his office, Donnell walked into his storefront and nodded to the two men helping a lady retrieve a document from an old hard drive. He'd started his own computer tech company a few years back, performing simple tasks like installing software programs, POS systems, and malware. Also working part-time as an independent operative with the CIA, Donnell spent most of his time behind a laptop. Over the last year, he'd stepped on a few toes in the CIA. The case involving Ashiree's kidnapping by Edward Morton opened up an investigation into a Colombian drug ring the CIA had been trying to bust for a few years. Darwin's now-fiancé Kelsey had a sex tape leaked by her cousin and a childhood friend of Darwin's attempting to sabotage Darwin and Kelsey's relationship earlier in the year. While removing the tape and having Kelsey's cousin arrested, the San Antonio officers stumbled upon a sex trafficking ring at the gentlemen's club Impressions, managed by Kelsey's aunt. Over seventy men and women were arrested and charged. Outside of the sex trafficking issue, Kelsey told Darwin about a trust fund set up by her late father that her aunt had been stealing money from. Evette Myers had stolen close to a quarter of a million dollars, just one-third shy of the trust funds' balance. The lawyer handling the embezzlement lawsuit was named Isaac Miller from Memphis, Tennessee. That case involved more than just illegal access to insurance policies, trust funds, and other investment securities.

The last and most recent incident involved a child abduction scandal surrounding Tricia Hanson. The case made him not so popular with the FBI, bringing shame onto the FBI's operating force. Tricia Hanson was presumed dead for over twelve years after a body was found in her car, burnt and unrecognizable. An accident with an oil tanker exploded on the freeway, causing a fifty-car pileup and several vehicles bursting into flames. The only problem was that Tricia Hanson had not been in the car, and the police report had not shown a person ejected from the vehicle before it exploded. Tricia discovered she had a sister, a twin sister, who required a kidney transplant. It was later determined that Tricia Hanson had been switched at birth by the woman she thought was her birth mother, Ailene Hanson. Ailene and her husband struggled to have a child. Their last efforts resulted in Ailene giving birth to a stillborn baby. She was desperate. As a nurse in the hospital, she had access to patients' rooms and could roam about the maternity ward without seeming suspicious. Another woman a few hours before had given birth to twin girls. Since the mother was a junkie and going into rehab, the babies would fall into the foster system. Ailene didn't see the point of both babies going to the foster system, so she made the switch. With the help of a few of her colleagues, the birth records and hospital documentation were altered and forged. In succeeding with the switch, they decided to expand into an operation, soliciting babies born from incarcerated women for private adoptions. This operation went on for nearly seven years until a doctor named Ruby Kerchel was killed. The FBI deemed the case closed, assuming Ruby had orchestrated the entire procedure by herself.

Closing the case made little sense to Donnell. Deciding to investigate himself, he reviewed mountains of old data and records, finding several inconclusive factors. He was puzzled why the FBI agent agreed to close it. After continuing his search, he came across the name of a man and paused. Donnell never forgot a name and was unsure as to why the name stuck out. He began searching through his other case files on his laptop until he found a hit. The name was under a folder he had on Ashiree when Dominic first discovered Ashiree might be pregnant with his child and requested a background check. Ashiree's record was clean outside of a few speeding tickets. Dominic had also asked Donnell to look into finding Ashiree's parents. The name Donnell found in searching the FBI case was the exact name of the lawyer that set up the private adoption for Ashiree.

The lawyer was connected to Ruby Kerchel by marriage. Piquing Donnell's curiosity further, he thought to search women's correctional facilities in the Boston Tri-City area, suspecting that the lawyer might have been involved in the child abduction ring. He came up short, and all the private adoptions set up by the lawyer appeared legal. None of the adoptions involved any interaction with

Ruby Kerchel. The women were young teens or college girls against abortion but didn't want to ruin their career paths by becoming mothers. Unable to stop himself, Donnell started looking into the night Ashiree was born. Three women had given birth that day, to two girls and a boy. What he found strange was the woman, listed as a Jane Doe, had an emergency c-section. The doctor listed on the patient paperwork was not an obstetrician but an Endocrinologist. Donnell found that strange and looked further into that doctor-patient record. The Endocrinologist was in the middle of testing patients with a rare count of white and red blood cells affecting the reproduction of cells in the body, specifically in the ovaries and thyroid glands. The research was practically unheard of. The current patients receiving treatment around that time were three men and four women. One of those women was Anita Campbell, the housekeeper and cook of his friend Dustin Shaw. She had been a professor of chemistry at Boston University and a widower nearing forty years old. Donnell didn't believe in coincidences. A tingling sensation pricked his neck when he looked into Anita's records as a professor. A glance at her class roster at Boston U revealed another name Donnell was familiar with, Austin Rollins. He knew from his discovery of Ashiree's brother last year that Austin Rollins was

Ashiree's father. There was an age difference of almost fifteen years between Anita and Austin and no proof of an affair. But the timing seemed too coincidental, and again, Donnell didn't believe in coincidences. He knew a simple phone call to Austin and a blood test between Ashiree and Anita would confirm or deny his suspicions.

Donnell rubbed his hand down his face; he was tired. He could never have predicted the events he'd stumbled upon in the last year and was still amazed at how things were unfolding all around him. Donnell logged onto his computer, checked his email, and saw the file of his next assignment. He'd been avoiding it for almost a month now and knew he could no longer put it off. Opening the file, he began to read the contents.

Chapter Three

Brandy finished wiping down the counters in the dining area, completely exhausted. The last two weeks were good for business. She had a steady round of customers coming daily, and she'd even received her first potential corporate client. A representative from Blake Enterprises emailed her to cater the dessert table for the upcoming Christmas party. After she'd blinked a few times to ensure the online order had been authentic, she squealed with delight. A client like Blake Enterprises would do wonders for her business.

"I am beat." Staci said, coming out of the kitchen after cleaning the espresso machine.

"Tired is a good thing." Brandy said, straightening the table and chairs.

"Business is picking up. You really should consider hiring someone." Staci suggested. Brandy had considered that. Staci could only help so much, and the work was getting a little too much for them.

"Do you think I should put up a 'Help Wanted'

sign?" Brandy asked.

"It wouldn't hurt, but the community college is a few blocks over. I'm sure there would be a few college kids that would like the job." Staci answered. Brandy nodded while coming behind the counter to clean the display case. She liked the idea of hiring a college student versus someone just walking in off the street.

"I might do that." she agreed.

"Great. Now, what are your plans this weekend?"

"Nothing planned so far." Brandy said sadly. She'd been so focused on getting the bakery up and running. She was working herself almost into exhaustion. She had enough time to check her email, eat a little something, shower, and then sleep. Only to get up the next day and do it all over again. The only day the bakery wasn't open was Sunday, and after Brandy slept in for a couple of hours, she would awake and spend most of the afternoon with her mother.

"Well Neely, Neil's sister, is here this weekend and wants to go to some birthday party." Staci announced.

"That sounds like fun." Brandy said, finishing cleaning the display case.

"I guess. She's young, still single, without a care in the world."

"We're not that old, Staci." Brandy said.

"Speak for yourself. I swear kids age you five extra years at a time." Brandy chuckled at Staci's complaint.

"Any who, do you think you can come out with us Saturday night?"

"For a birthday party? How old is this person?"

"Oh, I don't know. Neely mentioned it's for some ball player." Brandy quirked a brow.

"A ballplayer? Which one?"

"I can't remember. Hold on, let me text her."

"It doesn't matter. I'm sure it will be private." Brandy stated. Staci was texting and nodding her head. Brandy headed into the kitchen and tossed the rag in the sink. She began putting away her baking ware and utensils when Staci walked into the kitchen.

"Ok, so, the player is on the Houston baseball team. He's throwing himself a big party at a club downtown to make up for him canceling last year. Neely knows a few team members will be there and has a crush on the new rookie shortstop.

"I'm sure half the Houston population of women will try to get in." Brandy said.

"Neely says one of the bouncers can get us in." Brandy groaned. She'd grown out of her nightclub stage. Sports bars, or a nice lounge, was more her atmosphere these days.

"Is it just you and Neely?" Brandy asked.

"No, she and another friend, but I've been asked to be designated driver." Staci said with a slight eye roll.

"Can't Neil take her?" Brandy questioned.

"That was my suggestion, but Neely complained she couldn't flirt with any guys with her big brother acting as warden."

"I guess she has a point." Brandy said. Understanding Neil could definitely fit the overprotective brother type.

"Please, Brandy. I don't want to be the third wheel, and I know I will be completely bored with just Neely and her friend." Staci said with slightly pouting lips. Brandy shook her head at her silly plea.

"Fine, I'll help you chaperone." Brandy agreed.

"Thank you. Do you want us to stop by and pick you up?" Staci asked.

"Might as well, if you're playing DD, that means I get to drink ." Staci laughed at Brandy's words.

"Maybe you'll meet a ballplayer." Staci teased.

"Please, I like regular guys." Brandy said, shrugging her off. She finished the last of her cleaning a short while later and headed home.

"**Just how** many birthday parties does Damien plan on having?" Dexter asked.

"Last I heard, he was partying every weekend this month. Making up for last year." Dillon answered. Donnell shook his head in the back of Dexter's SUV. Last year on Damien's birthday, everyone was in a state of panic with Ashiree's kidnapping. And even after she was rescued, the desire to have a party was nonexistent. The three of them were heading to a nightclub in downtown Houston. The older club wasn't as popular as some newer ones; however, it held a greater capacity than most. Damien was opening up tonight's party to all who wanted to attend. As they exited I-59, Donnell could see the searchlights swirling around the sky, almost like a bat signal to locate the club.

"This is madness." Donnell said as Dexter rounded the corner to the club. Cars and vehicles were everywhere. Thankfully the Downtown streets were only one-way. Dexter pulled the SUV up to the valet, and the three of them exited the car.

"Hey, do you know if Dustin is coming?" Dillon asked.

"I believe so." Donnell answered just as the paparazzi attempted to storm the vehicle.

"Mr. Averitt, can we get a shot?"

"It's the Dex-It himself."

"Over here, Mr. Dex-It." Donnell followed Dexter as he promptly ignored the cameras and a few fans shouting his name. The bouncer immediately let them into the club and then escorted them to the VIP section designated for Damien's private guests. The inside of the club was massive, with three different stories, including the main floor. The music was loud, and people were everywhere. It took some pushing through the crowd for the bouncers to get them to a flight of stairs. Before they could begin their ascend, two ladies moved quickly past the bouncers to get a selfie with Dexter.

"Can you believe this? I would be over the top with the attention he gets." Dillon yelled. Donnell watched as Dexter, kindly as he could, took a few more shots before calling a halt to the crowd and began to walk up the stairs. Unlike the other side of the club, the flight of stairs only led to a second floor and a much larger private section. A waitress greeted them, not that Donnell could hear what she was saying with all the music. A couple of Damien's team members were already there. Donnell didn't know any of them, but Dexter and Dillon seemed to. A few of the players were clients that used most of Dexter's brand products for weightlifting and agility, while some had visited Dillon's sports bar, Quills. There was an oversized sectional that the three of them chose to sit on. The waitress took their drink order, and Donnell looked into the crowd below to see bodies gyrating to the beat and girls taking selfies. Most of the upper sections across the club seem to have a more private sitting area. He could make out tables and chairs but no one's faces. There was a bar for each floor, including one for their private section. Dillon and Dexter were laughing about something. Well, Dillon was laughing. Dexter gave his typical smirk. He hardly ever laughed out loud. The waitress brought their drinks just as he noticed Dustin and his wife coming up the stairs, followed by Darwin and Kelsey. They each stood, hugging one another in greeting.

"I'm surprised Tricia let you out of the house." Dillon teased Dustin as he took a seat next to his wife.

"He fulfilled his duty." Tricia answered, practically beaming at Dustin.

"Oh my gosh, does that mean you're pregnant?" Kelsey asked, her face wide with excitement. Tricia looked over at her and happily nodded.

"Congratulations." Kelsey squealed and leaned over to hug her.

"Way to go, Dust." Dillon said, throwing a fist bump at Dustin, which he happily returned. As the rest of them said their congratulations, a wild uproar surged from the crowd below. They all turned to glance down into the crowd as cheers arose, and the DJ changed the song, announcing Damien's arrival. The crowd parted like the red sea, allowing four waitresses holding champagne bottles with sparklers to lead Damien through. Camera flashes were everywhere, people were shouting his name, and he took several selfies before finally making it to the stairs.

"Forever the prima donna." Donnell heard Dexter say.

"Please, you had just as many women on you as he does now." Dillon responded.

"Maybe, but I don't enjoy it nearly as much as him." Dexter answered by watching Damien take another selfie before coming up the stairs. Once Damien hit the platform, he greeted his other team members, and Donnell finally noticed Shannon, Dominic and Ashiree behind him. They all greeted one another, and Dillon and Donnell moved over, allowing Damien to sit in the middle of the sectional.

"That was complete madness." Ashiree said.

"Honestly, that's pretty normal, wherever he goes." Dominic answered. A few of them nodded, knowing the full extent of Damien's popularity amongst Houstonians.

Brandy sipped her long island as the music thumped in the background. She was grateful the contact Neely had to get them into the club also provided them with a table. The abandoned warehouse didn't look like much from the outside, but the ambiance on the inside was spectacular. To their right, an entire decorative wall, going up to the ceiling was behind the main bar downstairs. The DJ Booth took up the wall to their left between them and the VIP section housed with second-floor access only, including its own private dance floor. They were currently on the second floor, on the other side of the club. Another floor was above them, and both held a private bar and a setup with tables, chairs, loungers, and hookah.

"Thank you so much for coming with me." Staci said, nudging her head at the third guy talking to Neely. Neely and her friend Cassie were both juniors in college, single and clearly ready to mingle. Brandy chuckled, knowing full well that if Neil had been there, there was no way he would allow the guy flirting with Neely anywhere near his sister.

"It's no problem. I'm actually happy I got out of the house." Brandy admitted.

"Yes! And you should get out more." Staci suggested.

"I know, I know, but the bakery takes up so much of my time. " Brandy said. It wasn't easy starting a new business.

"I get it, I do, but no work talk. Let's enjoy our night, chaperoning the kiddos." Staci said, lifting her glass. Brandy raised hers in a mock salute. Taking another sip, she looked down at the crowd of people below dancing, laughing and making their way over to the bar. It was a madhouse, and honestly, she missed this. During her own college days, she partied hard.

"Oh my gosh, he's here." Neely practically screamed as she and Cassie returned to the table. Looking over the railing, Brandy saw the crowd part as some people decided to take pictures.

"Who is that again?" Staci asked.

"That's the baseball team's newest member, Tavior Jonas." Neely began to explain.

"Yes, his sign-on contract was almost as big as the pitchers." Cassie added. They offered more information about the newest ball player as they watched him climb the stairs to the VIP section.

"I wish we could have gotten into the VIP section." Neely whined, seeing the object of her obsession.

"Sorry, this was the best I could do." Cassie explained.

"Well, your best was good enough for me. It definitely beats being down there." Staci said, pointing at the crowd below. There were no chairs or bar stools on the main floor. A few cocktail tables were in a section underneath them. The tempo of the music changed to Megan 'thee' stallion 'Savage' and the women in the club went crazy, singing over the music, loud, sassy, and proud of the Houston natives' success. Brandy and Staci laughed as both Cassie and Neely sang the words with animated head whipping, finger-pointing, and body curving. She had been the same in college when Beyonce played in the club. Neely and Cassie excused themselves after the song and headed to the ladies' room. Brandy and Staci went shortly after Neely and Cassie returned. Retaking their seats, a waiter brought a round of drinks when a slight uproar from the crowd caught their attention. A few new guests were entering the club.

"Brandy, isn't that Donnell?" Staci asked, puzzled. Brandy almost choked on her drink, looking over as the crowd parted.

"I'm not sure, but who is he with?" People were trying to get pictures of the man Donnell was walking behind.

"Oh my gosh, you two don't know who that is?" Neely said. Neely rolled her eyes. Both Brandy and Staci looked over at her and shook their heads.

"That's Dexter Averitt, Mr. Dex-it himself."

"The workout guy?" Staci questioned as they looked back over to see a few women blocking him from getting up the stairs to take pictures.

"You mean more like the workout god. I had to use my vibrator the last time I watched his workout video." Cassie admitted. Brandy looked over at her in shock.

"Sorry, she has no filter. So, you know the guy behind him?" Neely asked.

"He's one of my customers." Brandy answered, watching as the guys made it up the stairs and greeted the few ballplayers in the VIP section.

"Well, I've never seen him before, but I know the third guy with them. He owns sports bar we went to a few months back." Cassie said, directing her last statement to Neely.

"You're talking about Quills." Cassie nodded." That place was packed for the last fight." Neely added. Another song came on, prompting Neely and Cassie to dance as Brandy looked across the way at Donnell interacting with his friends. He was in the VIP section for Damien Storm's private birthday guest. Did Donnell know him personally?

Was he just a friend of a friend? He seemed like such a regular guy to have celebrities as friends. She may not keep up with all the stars and their lifestyles, but it was hard not to know about the ones that were Houston's own.

"I wonder who that is?" Neely said, shifting Brandy's gaze toward the stairs again.

"I'm not sure who the ladies are or the second guy with them, but the first one is Darwin Knight. My mother attends his fathers' church." Staci replied.

"It should be a shame for a preacher's son to look that good." Cassie sighed.

"You seriously have a thing for older guys." Neely accused.

"I have a thing for mature men. You can have these young guys if you want. I want someone with more stability and who is established.

"I hate to break it to you, but maturity doesn't always come with age." Staci commented. Brandy laughed and nodded in agreement. Looking back over at Donnell and his friend, Brandy heard Neely speaking aloud about making eye contact with her current baseball player obsession. Brandy ignored her as she focused on Donnell sitting on the extended sectional, leaning back while one of his ankles was resting on his knee. Even sitting, she could see the height difference from the others around him. Donnell looked casual, similar to how he dressed when he came into her bakery. He was dressed in a nice fitting burgundy polo shirt with black slacks and black shoes. He'd only visited her bakery once in the past week, which had been a slight disappointment. She rather enjoyed his presence and the slight flirtiness in his voice. Of course, she had to play indifferent around Staci. She didn't want her friend interfering more than she already had. The music changed again, causing another uproar in the crowd. Shouting, screaming, and cheering echoed off the walls as the man of the hour arrived.

"Ooo wee, the black Italian stallion has arrived." Neely chanted.

"Black Italian stallion?" Staci questioned, lifting a brow at Neely.

"Yes! That's his nickname. His mother is Black, and his dad is Italian." Staci shook her head at her sister-in-law.

"You seriously have a thing for ballplayers." Cassie said, throwing Neely's words back at her.

"Yes, I do, and I'm proud of it." Neely added. Four ladies with sparklers led the birthday man himself to the stairs. There were several delays in their approach to the stairs, as Damien Storm stopped to take several selfies with club goers. He finally made his way up the stairs and over to the group of friends with Donnell. Hugs and kisses on the cheeks were given to the ladies present, slaps on the back, and high fives between the men. Brandy watched the close-knit group. Damien acknowledged the group of teammates also present. He shared a shot with them, a few laughs before taking a seat in the middle of the big sectional.

"It seems your customer hangs out with some pretty high-end people." Cassie stated.

"Do you know the guy that came in with Damien?" Neely asked.

"No. I'm not sure who he is." Cassie admitted.

"Well, I'm assuming that's Dominic Blake." Staci answered.

"From Blake Enterprises?" Brandy asked. Staci nodded in confirmation. Brandy hadn't mentioned to Staci that Blake Enterprises asked her to cater desserts for the company Christmas Party.

"What makes you think that?" Neely asked, interrupting Brandy's thoughts.

"Well, for one, the woman that was behind Damien is Shannon Blake Walden. I remember watching her on the news cutting into some pretty nasty newscasters when the CFO from that pharmaceutical company was killed last year. Dominic Blake is her cousin."

"I think I heard about that. Wasn't his wife kidnapped or something?" Staci nodded her answer to Cassie's question.

"So, how close are you and this customer?" Neely asked Brandy.

"Not really close." Brandy admitted.

"They just flirt with one another, but he inquired about her single status." Staci said.

"No, you offered that information of your own free will." Brandy said, cutting eyes at her.

"So you're interested?" Neely asked with a sparkle in her eyes.

"Don't go there, Neely." Staci scorned.

"What?" she said innocently, shrugging her shoulders. "If she goes on a date with him, it wouldn't hurt if he used his connections so I can meet Tavior." Neely suggested.

"He hasn't asked me on a date." Brandy replied.

"And if he does...." Staci said, interrupting before Neely could speak. "...she will not placate him into getting you an introduction with your new crush." Neely pouted and looked over at Brandy. She shook her head and took another sip of her drink.

"Fine, you're such a party pooper." she whined to Staci." Let's go hit the dance floor." Neely suggested, grabbing Cassie by the hand and dragging her away.

"I'm so happy my parents only had one child." Staci joked. Brandy almost laughed with her but realized that wasn't true in her case. Taking another sip of her drink, she tried to block out Staci's words about being an only sibling and focused on watching Donnell laugh with his friends as they toasted to the birthday man.

Chapter Four

Donnell parked his car a few spaces down from Branded Flavors. He liked the play on words for her bakery's name. Working on the case, he was assigned to by Moore, proved to be a little more work than Donnell had expected. As a CIA operative, most of the data he analyzed was from foreign allies or enemies connected to several banks and financial institutions involved or played a role in large sums of cash making its way into the US. He would gladly pass the case onto the FBI to handle the domestic connections to prosecute if need be.

He entered the bakery, and the scent of cherry hit his nostrils. *Brandy's flavor of the day*, he thought. Instantly craving whatever treats she managed to concoct. It was fascinating what she could do with such a tiny dessert. The woman had an extraordinary talent, and Donnell became very interested in what other skills lay beneath. Flirting with her came easy. He did it without even trying. Her partner or friend gladly offered the information that she was single, and Donnell couldn't help but smile at Brandy's shocked expression from her friend's boldness. He wasn't sure if she was upset because her friend was interfering or if Brandy wasn't interested in him. The way Brandy looked at him, the way her words flowed from her lips as she spoke, oozed a sense of sensuality and attraction told him otherwise.

Staci was taking a coffee order as he stood in line behind a row of other customers. He didn't see Brandy. Once it was his turn, she happily greeted him.

"Good Morning. Donnell." She said,

"Good Morning. I smell cherry." He said with a smile.

"Yes, that is our flavor of the day." She said and extended her hand toward the display case. Donnell leaned over and selected two different pastries. He would surely need to hit the gym a little harder than usual. He already had a sweet tooth, and, in most cases, he could reign in his obsession with delectable sweets, but Brandy brought a whole new meaning to desserts for him.

"I'll take two of each." He pointed out.

"Alright." She said, grabbing a glove and a small paper bag.

"And where is our lovely baker this morning?" He asked.

"You just missed her. She had to run an errand.

Once the crowd dies down, I can normally handle the few customers we get after the morning rush." Staci answered while taking his card for payment. He nodded. That was the reason he came a little later than usual. As Staci called it, the morning rush prevented him from having any real interaction with Brandy other than a quick flirt. Something about his weekend changed his thoughts on asking her out. He was attracted to her, but he didn't always act on his attraction when it came to the women he encountered. Donnell liked a woman with talent, substance, and creativity. Brandy had all of that. While celebrating with his friends over the weekend, a slight longing developed inside of him. Damien, Dillon, and Dexter, were consummate bachelors and loving every minute. Dustin and Dominic happily married, Darwin on the path to join them, and Donnell somewhere in the middle.

Work took up most of his time, especially with the instances over the last year. He couldn't remember the last time he'd been on a date. Maybe a year ago? It was shortly after attending Dominic's grandfather's funeral. He, Dexter, Damien, and Dillon, met up with Dominic at Quills. He remembered seeing the stress Dominic was going through and couldn't imagine the pain he was feeling. He knew what it was like to lose his grandfather, but Donnell still had his parents. He'd sensed Dominic's sorrow and his worry. Remembering them all being together Saturday night, he couldn't help but smile as he noticed Dominic completely happy with his wife, celebrating Damien's birthday and enjoying them all being together. Donnell had felt it too. It was the thing he really liked about Ashiree. She wanted to keep them all close and continued to host dinner every Thursday evening at Blake manor. She was turning Blake Manor back into a home for Dominic. He'd vowed not to live there again after his grandmother died and had not returned until the death of his grandfather. The weight of the family and its legacy now fell on his shoulders. Ashiree helped him carry that burden, allowing Dominic the opportunity to enjoy his life. Donnell wanted that. He wanted it for the first time in his life and decided to pursue Brandy. She was the first woman in a long time to truly pique his interest.

"I'm sorry I missed her." He said, bringing his thoughts to a halt and accepting both his card and his bag of treats from Staci.

"I'll be happy to give her a message for you." Staci prompted. He smiled, knowing Staci was indeed into helping play matchmaker between him and her friend.

"Give her this for me," He said, handling Staci a business card. "My cell number is on the back." He watched as Staci looked at the card, turned it over in her hand to verify his cell number was there before turning it over again.

"You're a tech guy." She said, not asking but still looking at his card.

"Among other things." Donnell admitted.

"I thought you were some hot-shot businessman." Staci said, finally looking back at him.

"Nope, just a regular guy." He confirmed.

"With some pretty influential friends." Donnell's eyebrow lifted at her words. "We saw you Saturday night at the birthday party for Damien Storm."

"Ah." He said, nodding in understanding. "His one of many." Donnell added, smiling.

"Yes, I heard he had two other parties."

"You heard right." Donnell confirmed, not offering any information why Damien needed to have three separate birthday parties.

"Well, I will give this to Brandy and, I will make sure she calls you." Donnell smiled.

"I would appreciate that. You have a good day, Staci." He said, backing away from the counter.

"You have a good one as well, Donnell." She replied, shaking his card in her hand. He couldn't help the smile displayed on his face as he left and headed for his car.

Brandy wanted to leap for joy as she left the thirteen-story building of Blake Enterprises. After receiving the online order, she made an appointment to speak to the event coordinator for the upcoming Christmas party. Notepad in hand, she jotted down various details on desserts that had been catered in the past. She also brought a portfolio and a few samples to give her bakery an extra spark in Blake Enterprises' decision to hire her. The person handling the event was the administrative assistant to Shannon Blake Walden. His name was Ramone, and he was very detailed and particular in letting her know how grand this year's Christmas party would be. The Christmas party last year had been canceled because of the CEO's family recovering from the kidnapping of his wife. Brandy also learned that the Blake family had also lost their patriarch only five months earlier. She recalled seeing Dominic and Ashiree Blake at the club on Saturday. After attending church with her mother and finally returning home, she googled the couple and found their interview last year on YouTube. Brandy was almost in tears listening as the couple not only told their love story but hearing the genuine fear in Ashiree's voice as she recanted the experience of her kidnapping. Ashiree solemnly expressed her worry regarding an unknown drug she had been injected with by her kidnappers and the effects it could have on their unborn child. Brandy also learned that Mr. and Mrs. Blake delivered a healthy baby boy almost six months ago named Arion.

Finding her car in the parking garage, she held the stamped parking ticket and handed it to the parking attendant as she left the Downtown garage. Houston traffic was at an all-time high, as she slowly made her way down I-59. She turned on her Apple Music and allowed the melody of her playlist to soothe her while creeping through traffic. A twenty-minute ride back to her bakery turned into a little over an hour, and Brandy was excited to share her news with Staci. Parking in the back of her bakery, she saw the lady next door that owned a small boutique tossing a box in the dumpster.

"Hi Lisa." She called out as she parked and exited her vehicle.

"Hi Brandy." She said, dusting off her hands as she made her way over to Brandy from the dumpster.

"How are things going?" Brandy asked, reaching in her backseat to grab her portfolio and notepad.

"Going well; I see you have brought some business to our little shopping center." Lisa stated. The shopping center only consisted of eight stores. Lisa rented two for her boutique, and to the right was a hardware store. Branded Flavors was on the left of the boutique, next to a nail salon and then a sandwich shop. The last two units were vacant. They chatted for a minute about business.

"I do what I can." Brandy replied. When Brandy first met Lisa, she instantly liked her. It was nice to see another young black woman pursuing their dreams. Lisa's family designed clothes. Lisa herself created jewelry and other trinkets. She had a successful online business before finally opening up her own location. She and Brandy's stories were similar; only Brandy intended to be a chef and discovered her natural talent was actually in desserts. After her quick chat with Lisa, Brandy headed into the back of her bakery, unlocked the door with her key, and announced her arrival ensuring she did not scare Staci.

"Staci, I'm back." She called out and locked the door behind her, placed her portfolio and notepad down on the small desk in the back room.

"Hey. How did your meeting go?" Staci asked, wiping down the island in the kitchen as Brandy walked in.

"Very good. We have our first corporate client."

"Really? And who is it?"

"Blake Enterprises!" Brandy almost shouted. Staci's jaw dropped.

"What? Oh my gosh! That's so great. How?"

"I don't know. They put in an inquiry order last week, and I set up a meeting."

"And you're just now telling me?" Staci asked.

"I didn't want to get my hopes up. It's a major client."

"I know. Hey, do you think Donnell had anything to do with it?" Staci asked. Brandy's eyebrows hunched; she hadn't considered that. Not that it mattered. But now that she thought about it, maybe he had said something to Mr. Blake. After seeing the close-knit group on Saturday, the idea wasn't far-fetched.

"Well, if he did, I might have to thank him." Brandy said, slightly shrugging her shoulders.

"I think you should." Staci said with a sly smile on her face.

"What does that look mean?" Brandy asked curiously.

"Oh nothing." She began while reaching in the back pocket of her jeans. "Except someone left their card for you to call them." She continued, handing the card to Brandy. Brandy took it in unbelief and read it. There it was in bold letters: his name, title, company name, and email address. Staci motioned for her to turn the card over, and on the back was his cell phone number. Donnell wanted her to call him? She grew skeptical and glanced back up a Staci.

"Did you bribe him for this?" she asked. Staci laughed.

"No, not that I wouldn't have, but he honestly came in like fifteen minutes after you left. I think he wanted to catch you when the morning rush was over." Brandy nodded her head. That was why she had scheduled her meeting with Blake Enterprises in the early afternoon. From six in the morning until almost noon, she was completely swamped.

"Do you think I should call?"

"You already know my answer to that. But if it helps, I think he's really into you, Bran." Staci said. Brandy twirled the card around in her hand. When was the last time a guy had been really into her?

"I'll think about it." Brandy stated. Staci rolled her eyes, and Brandy asked about the rest of the afternoon. Staci filled her in, reminding her to post the flyer at the college for some help.

Donnell almost missed the call coming through on his phone. He rarely kept his ringer on. Not recognizing the number, he decided to answer it, anyway.

"This is Donnell."

"Hi." A voice said on the other end. Donnell didn't recognize it.

"Who is this?" he asked. The voice told him, and shock hit him.

"Hi, how are you?" Donnell asked.

"I'm doing alright. You told me I could call you when I was ready."

"I did, and I meant it."

"I think I'm ready, well, actually, I've been ready, but I was trying to be understanding of the situation."

"I get that." Donnell answered.

"So, how should we do this?" the voice asked.

"I'll need to talk with her first."

"Oh." The voice said, defeat etching in the single word.

"Don't worry. I'm sure she'll be thrilled. She's wanted this for a while."

"My parents don't know I'm calling." The voice admitted.

"Are you coming alone?"

"Yes, the twins are still too young to make this decision on their own. Things are still pretty tense between all of us."

"I understand. What day did you have in mind?"

Donnell asked.

"Any day. I'm open to whatever is good for her."

"Alright, I'll set something up soon and let you know."

"That would be great."

"And Ashden?" Donnell said before allowing him to hang up.

"Yes."

"Thanks for calling." Donnell said before disconnecting the call.

Brandy grabbed the glass of wine she'd just poured and went to stand on her balcony outside her apartment. From her balcony, she could see a pond encompassed by the other apartment buildings. There were only four units to a building, each with its private garage and a walkway out to the pond. The community was small, and most of her neighbors were single or couples with no children. A few were currently running around the track surrounding the pond with their partners or pets.

Brandy took a sip from her glass, sat on her small settee on the balcony, and watched as a couple waved as they passed by. They lived in the building unit next to her, and she saw them often when arriving home from the bakery. She liked how they were always together. Walking, jogging, even working out in the community gym on the property. It made her wonder for a minute if she would have that type of relationship with a man. Her neighbors looked like friends more than just lovers, and Brandy wondered if that were truly possible.

Taking another sip then placing her glass on the small table in front of her, she took a deep breath and let her thoughts wander to the one man that seemed to pique her interest. She did her best not to allow daydreams of him. Trying to keep her mind focused on continuing to build and manage the bakery. That was never easy with Staci around, constantly finding it easy to enter Donnell into their conversation. She knew Staci meant well and wanted her to date and find a good man. Staci had gotten lucky with Neil. From the moment they'd met at the restaurant, Neil only had eyes for her. Staci was not an easy task for men's wooing ways, and she did not make it easy for Neil. But Brandy, having grown up slightly thicker than most girls, recalled the unpleasant teasing and mocking in high school. However, college changed all that. The myth of boys or men being unattracted to full-figured women was proven wrong. They couldn't seem to keep their eyes off her. From the new school jocks to the engineers to the so-called science geeks, she'd experienced them all. Her issue was that she didn't trust men—the idea of happily ever after was shot dead by her own parents' marriage. Staci had told her plenty of times that parents get divorced, people change, grow apart, and all the other beautiful excuses that came about with a couple getting divorced, but Staci didn't know all of it.

Grabbing her glass again, she took another sip and then exhaled. She seriously considered calling or texting Donnell last night. But her decision was interrupted by the friend request she'd received. She wasn't sure how long she'd stared at the name before finally declining it. Brandy wasn't ready, and she wasn't sure if she would ever be ready. The constant reminder that her world had fallen apart, life as she'd known it was a lie, was something she honestly didn't want to deal with. She was being childish in some ways, and she was aware of it. Plenty of people found out they had a sibling, and despite the origin of how those siblings came to be, that did not deter others from having a relationship with them. But Brandy wasn't one of those people. For years, she hid behind the hurt, pain, devastation, and embarrassment it had caused her mother, but she could admit now, it just kept her relationship with her father strained. A part of her wanted to go back to the little girl that adored her father, where she had been daddy's princess, a title she believed was only held by her. Lies, all lies. Her sister, who was only a few months younger, was also daddy's princess. Maybe she'd feel different if the love child from her father's ongoing affair had been a boy. Brandy wasn't sure. All she knew was that she had felt special, important, the apple of her father's eye, and it had all been a lie.

Finishing the contents of her drink, she allowed herself a few more minutes of self-wallowing before she noticed the sun beginning to descend. Standing and stretching, she walked back into her apartment, placed her glass in the kitchen sink, and headed to her bedroom. She grabbed her phone off the nightstand and breathed a sigh of relief when she didn't see any notification for another friend request. Her mother texted her a couple of times, and Staci also had. She quickly responded to her mother and then rolled her eyes, reading Staci's texts about reaching out to Donnell. Brandy almost answered but decided it was none of Staci's business, knowing that would drive her friend crazy. Heading for the shower, still pondering whether she wanted to reach out to Donnell.

Chapter Five

Donnell parked his car, grabbed the bag in the passenger seat, and walked up the drive of the two-story home. Hearing the commotion from the backyard, he bypassed the front walkway and headed around the side of the house. Opening the back gate to the backyard, he saw a few tables and chair settings with balloons tied at the ends.

"Donnie, you made it." He heard his aunt Melinda say. He walked over and embraced her with a hug. Technically, she was no longer his aunt; once she and his uncle divorced, but his grandmother insisted she was present for family functions.

"It's good to see you. And I actually brought a gift this time." Donnell said, handing her the gift bag in his hand. Melinda laughed as she took the gift bag from him.

"I'm sure your grandmother will love it." She took the gift over to the table with other presents. He followed.

"Where is Grandma Judy?" Donnell asked.

"You know she has to make a grand entrance. I'm

sure Megan is helping her get ready now." Donnell nodded while speaking to the other party attendees.

"Is Dillon here yet?" He asked his aunt Melinda.

"Oh, I'm sure he's at Quills taking care of a few things." Melinda responded.

"He is always at Quills taking care of a few things." The dry tone shifted Donnell's gaze to the table with his uncle and parents.

"Don't start, Alvin. Today is about your mother." Melinda warned her ex-husband.

"Donnie, it's so good to see you." his mother said, ignoring her brother-in-law's comment and standing slowly to hug him. He had to crouch down quite a bit to accommodate her height. He kissed her cheek before releasing her.

"How are you feeling, mom?"

"Not too bad for an old woman." Francine Mason said.

"But a beautiful one." his father complimented, making his mother blush.

"How are you, pops?" Donnell said, leaning down to hug his father.

"Oh, if it weren't for this body, I'd live forever." Milton Mason said, chuckling.

"Uncle Alvin." Donnell addressed his uncle with a

former handshake. Alvin Mason was not a man to hug or embrace.

"It's good to see you, Donnell." he said, accepting the firm handshake. Donnell took a seat at the table and talked with his parents. He watched, as he always did, how they interacted with one another. His father still held his mother's hand, still smiled lovingly at her, and complimented her constantly. They were older than most of his friends or cousins' parents. His dad was nearly forty when he was born. His mother, being older than his father, was in her mid-forties. They had almost given up on having a child. Then when they least expected, his mother was pregnant with him. It worked out well. His aunt Melinda found out she was pregnant only a few weeks after his mother, allowing him and Dillon the close relationship they had now.

The back gate opened, and Dillon walked through, all smiles announcing his presence. His mother quickly made her way over to him and hugged him. Dillon picked her up and spun her around once.

"Forever with the theatrics, that son of mine." Donnell heard Alvin say. "It's amazing he didn't go into acting." Alvin continued.

"Why? Is that a profession you would have approved of?" His dad said. Donnell watched his uncle side-eye his older brother but didn't answer. There was still some bad blood between the brothers since Dillon decided to walk away from a corporate job and take over the bar when Donnell's father was confined to a wheelchair. Milton Mason, like Dillon, loved the sports bar opened by their grandfather. It was a long-standing source of income for them when they were children. Dillon's father had not been quiet about his disapproval of Dillon taking over Quills. He saw it as a waste of time and money, with the intellect Dillon had. A few years back, his verbal expression caused a slight rift in the relationship with his older brother.

Dillon made his way over to their table with his mother, speaking to others in attendance to celebrate their grandmother's 90th birthday. Most were from her church and bingo club.

"Hey, dad." Dillon greeted his father. He stood and extended his hand. Dillon took it but quickly grabbed him in for a hug. Alvin stood stiff and slightly uncomfortable before Dillon released him and spoke to Donnell and his aunt and uncle. The back door to the house opened and Megan's husband, Scott, exited holding their one-year-old son and four-year-old daughter's hand. The moment little Markle saw Dillon, she beelined straight for him.

"Uncle Dillon!" she cried, arms out as she ran

toward him.

"How's my warrior princess?" Dillon said, scooping her up in his arms.

"Mommy is putting a lot of color on GG Judy." Markle said, trying to whisper, but everyone could hear her.

"Does she look like a clown?" Dillon asked, faking to whisper as well. Markle shook her head.

"No, she looks like a queen." she answered proudly. Dillon smiled, putting her down as Scott made his way over with Scott Jr., that they all called SJ. Scott greeted everyone, handing SJ off to his mother-in-law. They all sat at the long picnic table, waiting for their grandmother to make her entrance. Not one to disappoint, Judith Mason soon made her appearance looking stylish in a powder blue floral dress, the sleeves flowing just below her elbow and the hem gracing at her calves. She wore flat sandals and thanked everyone for coming and the good lord for the nice weather. Megan walked out right behind her, pride in her grandmother's appearance and attire showing on her face. Their grandmother made her way over to greet her friends while Megan made her way over to them.

"Donnie, it's so good to see you." she said. Donnell stood and hugged Megan.

"Nice to see you too, Megan." he said before releasing her.

"Dillon, it is so nice of you to grace us with your presence." she said, teasing her brother.

"What's a party without me?" Dillon said with a wink. She rolled her eyes, giving a side hug to her brother and making her way around the other side of the table to sit next to her husband.

"Don't look now, but Grandma Judy is talking to Mrs. Parks." Megan said.

"Is there something wrong?" Donnell asked.

"Not really, but Grandma Judy had another fish dream last night, and she believes Mrs. Parks' daughter is pregnant."

"And that's a bad thing?" Dillon questioned.

"For Mrs. Parks, yes. She has made it known that she does not wish to be a grandmother."

"Maybe Grandma Judy is wrong?" Dillon offered.

"Well, from what I've seen, your grandmother has been spot on. At least with my sister and us." Scott said.

"That seems to be the case, although I think she's been off at least once." Megan admitted. Both Donnell and Dillon turned their heads toward her.

"When was this?" Donnell asked. For as far back as he could remember growing up, every time his grandmother had a fish dream, someone in their close circle was pregnant. His grandmother had been spot on, as Scott said, and not once had he ever heard that she'd had a Fish dream and someone didn't admit to being pregnant within a week.

"If you're talking about the one from last year, no, she was spot on. It was Dominic." Dillon said before Megan responded.

"I figured that one out, but this one was years ago. I was still in high school. Momma or auntie Francey don't seem to remember." Megan stated.

"But you do?" Dillon asked skeptically.

"Yes, my best friend at the time had just lost her virginity to her boyfriend, and I was scared to death. You know momma told me if I had sex, I would get pregnant." Megan admitted. Dillon laughed, and even Scott chuckled.

"So, was your friend pregnant?" Donnell asked.

"No, and that was puzzling to me. Grandma Judy is known for her Fish dreams. But no one was pregnant until months later after she had another one. Heck, at one point, I thought either you or Dillon might come home from college announcing you'd got some girl pregnant." Donnell chuckled, and Dillon scuffed. They all looked back over at Mrs. Parks' distressed expression, almost as if she was confirming his grandmother's words. That seemed weird to Donnell. All the mothers he knew couldn't wait to find out they were going to be grandparents.

"So, what's going on with you and the baker?" Dillon questioned, interrupting his thoughts.

"What baker?" Megan asked, slightly intrigued.

"Donnie here is obsessed with a baker." Dillon said, pointing his thumb at Donnell.

"I'm not obsessed. But I'm interested." Donnell admitted. He wasn't the type of man to hide when he was interested in a woman. He honestly didn't find many women he was interested in, which instantly made Brandy different.

"Well, what's she like?" Megan inquired. Donnell spent the next few minutes talking about Brandy, her bakery, and him wanting to take her to dinner. Shortly after, the conversation switched over to Megan and Scott buying a house and the family plans for the upcoming holidays, before it was time to sing happy birthday to their grandmother.

"**So, did** you call him yet?" Staci asked, entering the bakery kitchen as Brandy was mixing the batch of today's special.

"No, I didn't." Brandy admitted.

"What are you waiting for? It's not like you're not interested." Brandy exhaled a breath and kept turning the bowl as she whipped the contents inside. She knew she was interested, and that was the problem.

"Ignoring the question won't make it go away." Staci pushed. Brandy smiled.

"Why are you so interested in my love life?" Brandy asked.

"Well, it's nothing going on in mine, so yours is open for discussion." Brandy paused from her stirring and looked over at Staci.

"Trouble in paradise?" she asked.

"No, just Neil's mother being at the house is killing my sex drive." Brandy quirked a brow.

"How?"

"The guest room downstairs flooded when a pipe burst in the bathroom. We have to get all new piping throughout the entire downstairs of the house, but that is another issue. Anyway, the only other available bedroom is the one upstairs next to Neil and mine."

"Why is that a problem?" Brandy asked.

"Because Neil doesn't want his mother to hear us having sex."

"Then maybe you shouldn't be so loud, Staci." Brandy teased.

"I'm not the loud one. Neil is." Staci countered.

"How long does she plan to stay?"

"It was only supposed to be for a couple of weeks. Now she is talking about selling her house and moving in with us."

"Is she that bad?"

"No, especially not compared to other mother-in-laws, but it's my house Brandy, my children, and my husband. I don't want to feel like I have to explain my choices or decisions when it comes to my family." Staci complained.

"Did you tell Neil this?"

"I tried. He just sees it as a good thing not to have to pay for a babysitter. Since we work different schedules and I'm here in the mornings."

"Oh, Staci, I can focus more on getting someone in here to help me. I don't want to cause a problem with you two."

"You're not Brandy. I promise I'm just venting. I should be grateful. It keeps a lot more money in our household with her there.

"Maybe, but the tradeoff of added stress doesn't seem to help."

"Neither does the lack of sex, which brings me back to you."

"What does sex have to do with me?" Brandy asked.

"Well, if you stop stalling and get with a certain customer that's interested in you, I can hear sex stories."

"Staci, you are crazy, but I love you."

"Love me enough to call Donnell. Seriously, one of us in this room needs to be having sex."

"I think the married one in the room needs to wear that title." Brandy said, laughing.

"One would think." Staci replied dryly. Brandy shook her head and changed the subject to the dessert ideas for the Blake Christmas party. Staci helped her organize her thoughts and put together a theme and potential display for the event. Brandy had goosebumps in excitement. This was a significant account and, if done successfully, would open many doors for corporate clients in the future.

Once, the morning rush died down after they opened. Staci needed to run home, and Brandy thought about Donnell. He hadn't visited her bakery all week. She looked forward to seeing him and missed their subtle flirting. Had he not come because she hadn't called? Deciding to put her big girl panties on and find out, Brandy reached inside the pocket of her apron and grabbed her phone. She'd already saved his cell number. *Call or Text*, she thought. He might not answer her call if he was busy. She decided to send a text. But what should she send? He didn't have her number, so she couldn't just send 'hi' like a random person. Or maybe 'hi, this is brandy', but that seemed so generic. Why did these things have to be so complicated? She wanted him to know it was her without outright telling him. Biting the inside of her cheek, Brandy turned her phone over in hand as her palms began to sweat. She stopped as a thought entered her mind. Before losing the nerve to do so, she sent the text and quickly put it back in her pocket as she heard the bell on the door chime. Anticipating his response as she helped her customer, she didn't have to wait as long before she felt the vibration of her phone in her apron, a sign a message was received. She smiled harder than needed and thanked her customer. Nerves in a bunch, Brandy waited for them to exit and then pulled her phone back out to check her message.

Donnell placed his phone down on his desk, waiting for Brandy to respond. He'd almost ignored the incoming message. Donnell was working on tracing money back to the United States from an unknown source. Once he could pinpoint where the money was distributed, he would turn it over to the FBI. His phone beeped again, and he checked for Brandy's response. She flirted a little about him missing her daily theme with pineapples. *The things that woman did with food.* She intrigued him, not only with her talent for making delectable desserts but the passion behind her talent. When she spoke about her daily or weekend-themed desserts, her eyes lit, her slow and steady smile filled with appreciation and pride. He wanted to know more about her. When her friend Staci mentioned they were at the club for Damien's birthday, he replayed the scoop of the layout of the club in his mind and tried to picture what area Brandy had been in. He resolved to think she had been on the second or third level across from the VIP section where they'd sat. He'd scanned the bottom floor of the club several times and would have recognized her, even in a crowd of people. An email popped up on his computer, taking his attention away from his text back and forth with Brandy. He texted her, asking if he could call her later, and she responded with a good time for her. Quickly opening the email, he read the encrypted text, jotted down the address, and deleted it. It was oddly chilly for Houston in mid-November, so he grabbed his jacket. Checking on the guys at the front of the store, he told them he would be back in a couple of hours. They casually replied, and Donnell headed out to his car.

Brandy walked into her apartment, plopped onto her couch, tossed her purse, and quickly discarded her shoes. Rubbing her feet, she fully understood her grandmother having a mini foot soaker in her home, and Brandy might have to consider getting the same. Or maybe a pedicure. She couldn't remember the last time she'd taken the time out to do some pampering. After rubbing her feet a minute longer, she laid her head back on the sofa and sighed in contentment. She was exhausted and needed to get some help. Done with putting it off, she stood, mildly stretched, and headed to her bedroom. Grabbing and opening her laptop, she found the email from the counselor at the nearby community college. She filled out the requested form for any culinary students on campus who might want to work part-time at her bakery. She was currently opening the bakery every other Saturday, and she would love to change that. But there was only so much she could do on her own. Starting out, Brandy couldn't predict the demand or steady flow of customers visiting her business. But now, almost two months in, she needed to address her staffing issues. She'd also received confirmation from Blake Enterprises and the deposit she'd requested to accept the order. The butterflies dancing in her stomach when she thought of the contract she'd landed could not be contained. She was a small business, practically nobody of any real popularity in the industry, and Blake Enterprises allowed her to cater their Christmas Party. Her thoughts shifted to what Staci mentioned about Donnell maybe having something to do with that. A slow smile graced her face as she recalled texting with him earlier. There was nothing unique or excessive, just some light flirting and food innuendos. The man truly had a sweet tooth. He'd joked about having to hit the gym a few more times in the last couple of weeks because of her desserts. She quickly checked the time, remembering when she'd told him a good time to call her. She had about an hour. Finishing the work-form and sending it off, she put her laptop on her mini desk and headed for the shower.

Donnell nodded as the caddy driver dropped him off at the thirteenth hole. Moore was bending down to place his ball on the tee. Donnell wasn't a golf player, but the slight gust of wind that blew passed as he walked over to Moore let him know he was about to swing into the wind. The one thing Donnell assumed going well for Moore, was that the sun was behind him. Once Moore lined up his putter and took his shot, he turned to see Donnell.

"Glad you could make it, Mason."

"Your email didn't seem like a suggestion." A sly smile showed on Moore's face. He knew it hadn't been.

"I heard you're planning on leaving the CIA." Moore said, not beating around the bush or engaging in small talk.

"That's not something I'm hiding from anyone. You know I never planned to be involved this long." Donnell admitted. He'd been a CIA operative for eight years, gathering foreign intel whenever they needed him to. It had been his first job after college. The timing had worked out perfectly, since shortly after his dad had gotten into a major accident preventing his ability to walk. He needed the money to take on some of his parents' bills before insurance, and the lawsuit money paid out.

"I need you to reconsider." Moore stated, flatly, bending down again to pick up his tee. Donnell placed his hands in his jacket pockets and blew out a breath.

"I'm sure you're going to tell me why."

"Walk with me." Moore suggested, walking toward where his ball landed, with every intention of Donnell following him. Donnell watched as Moore lined his putter to swing again.

"They are pushing me out, Mason." He said, just before taking his swing. Donnell lost sight of the ball as the meaning of Moore's words hit him.

"Pushing you out? Why?" Donnell asked, unnerving concern etched in his voice.

"They're not too happy about the mission in Venezuela." Donnell nodded, remembering hearing about it. He hadn't worked with Moore on intel for that mission. The information given to the pentagon had been corrupted. The result had been six marines killed, the wrong assailant assassinated, and an American woman's body parts mailed home to her family. Covering up the complete failure of the mission was a nightmare.

"What does that have to do with me?"

"I need someone I trust on the inside." Moore said, finally looking over at Donnell. His eyebrow hunched. *Who was Moore trying to protect?* Donnell quickly went over mission and covert operations intel in his mind before a name stuck out.

"Archer?" Donnell asked, already knowing the answer before he saw Moore nod.

"He's not really AWOL, is he?" Donnell asked.

"Officially, yes, unofficially, no." Moore answered.

"Where is he?"

"Not sure. We lost track of him a couple of weeks

ago."

"Where was he last?"

"Somewhere in the DR." Moore answered.

"Is he in danger?" Donnell asked.

"If he stays away, no." Donnell blew out a breath and stared back at Moore.

"If you want me to stay and keep a lookout for Archer, tell me everything about the mission in Venezuela. Even the intel you're not supposed to know." An odd smile appeared on Moore's face, but he soon nodded and turned to walk toward the next hole. Again expecting Donnell to follow, and he did, as Moore told him everything.

Chapter Six

Brandy wrapped her towel around her as she stepped out of the shower. There was no better feeling than washing off the day with a nice hot shower. She loosened the tie that was holding her goddess braids up and let them fall over her shoulder. She loved the look of them. She wasn't brave enough to lock her own hair into dreads, so goddess locs would have to do. Grabbing her signature lavender lotion off her vanity, she discarded her towel and began to lather her body. The scent started to fill the room as she continued working the lotion into her skin. Brandy opened her drawer, pulled out a nightgown, and placed it over her head. She loved the smooth satin falling over her skin down to her calves. Heading to the kitchen, Brandy bit the inside of her jaw at the few leftovers she had stashed and decided she wanted Mexican food. Grabbing the phone, she noticed the time and realized Donnell hadn't called yet. Shrugging her shoulder, she opened her UberEATS app and placed an order. Surprisingly, the wait for her food wouldn't be long. Just as she sat on her couch and turned on the TV, her phone rang. Her nerves shot up seeing Donnell's name on the screen.

"Hello." she answered as calmly as she could.

"Good Evening Ms. Brandy." The man's voice sounded smooth like butter.

"Good Evening, Donnell."

"How are you?" He asked. She shifted one leg under her on the couch.

"I'm doing pretty well. How about yourself?"

"Not too bad, pleased I finally get a chance to talk with you." she chuckled, then heard traffic sounds in the background.

"Are you in your car?" she asked.

"I am. Heading toward my condo."

"Oh, what part of Houston do you live in?" He told her, and she nodded. He lived in a very nice area. She thought about the distance from his place to the bakery, and it was almost forty minutes away. That was the crazy thing about how big Houston was. You could live nearly an hour away and still be in Houston.

"Brandy?" She heard him call her name.

"I'm here." she said, realizing her thoughts had taken her away from the conversation.

"I thought I lost you." he said, his voice laced with slight concern.

"No, I just got lost in thought. The bakery is far from where you live."

"Ah, I see. No, the bakery isn't close to where I live. It's closer to where a friend of mine lives." he responded.

"You must visit your friend a lot." she teased. She heard him chuckle.

"Or I don't mind burning up gas to see a very special baker."

"Donnell, are you flirting with me?" she knew he was, but she liked the slight tease.

"If you have to ask, I'm doing a terrible job at it." she laughed at his comment just as there was a knock on her door.

"Hold on, someone is at my door."

"Are you expecting someone?" he asked, his tone seeming on alert.

"Yes, I ordered food." she answered.

"Keep the phone with you." she quirked a brow at his request but shrugged it off and answered her door. She thanked the delivery guy, informed him that his tip was added when she paid, then closed her door and locked it.

"I have my food safe and sound." she announced as she walked over to her dining area. Placing her bag on her small round glass table, she headed to her kitchen for a plate and silverware. Eating out of plastic containers or with plastic utensils just made her cringe.

"I'm glad. What did you order?"

"Enchiladas." she stated, taking a seat in her dining room. Her original plan for tacos shifted when she was going through the app, deciding what to order.

"So, you like Mexican food? I'll keep that in mind for our first date."

"Are you asking me or telling me we're going on a date?" she asked, somewhat teasing. In all honesty, she didn't like it when a man assumed she would agree without some pushback, but Donnell didn't speak to her with a tone of arrogance or cockiness.

"Definitely telling. I'm not allowing you the opportunity to tell me no." he said with a slight chuckle in his voice.

"And if I still refuse?" she asked.

"I'll bring in reinforcements." he answered. Brandy paused for a minute before realizing who he was talking about. She smirked. Staci.

"You have turned my best friend against me." she said playfully.

"Whatever works, but I'll let you eat your dinner and call you tomorrow."

"Alright, good night, Donnell."

"Good night, Brandy." he replied before

disconnecting their call.

Ashiree Blake paced around her sitting room. Earlier, Donnell's call should have had her leaping for joy, but all it did was put her in a fit of nerves. Her brother wanted to meet her. She waited almost a year to hear that and nearly her whole life to know she wasn't alone. Growing up in the foster system left old scars of loneliness and feelings of being unwanted and unloved. She'd overcome all of that, determined never to let her upbringing stop her from living life, exploring every opportunity she could, and having no regrets.

"You're nervous." Ashiree turned to the voice of her husband as he entered the sitting room. She smiled as he approached her, placing his arm around her waist to bring her close to him. She never thought she'd be the girl to get goosebumps or butterflies in her stomach around a man. The girl who believed in fairytales and happily ever after was never her, but here she was, living out a true fairytale with her husband.

"A little." She admitted, resting into his embrace, taking in the scent of his musky cologne, and looking into his brown eyes. A sly smile formed with his lips as the dimple in his left cheek, that she loved so much, appeared.

"Everything will work out. Don't worry." Dominic reassured her as he kissed her forehead. He seemed so unreal at times, enduringly sweet, unapologetically affectionate, and meticulously understanding.

"That's easier said than done." She admitted. He brought her fully into his embrace and leaned down to give her a chaste kiss.

"I'm right here if you need me." He said, and she believed him. That was something she never had to worry about.

"Thank you." She replied, leaning up to kiss him back.

"Mr. and Mrs. Blake," They both turned as Marvin appeared in the entryway. "Your guests have arrived." He announced.

"Thank you, Marvin," Dominic answered before looking back down at Ashiree. "Do you want to meet him in here?" he asked her. She bit her lip before taking a deep breath and nodded.

"Please send them in, Marvin." Ashiree said, taking a slight step out of Dominic's arms. He took her hand and kissed it.

"Relax." Dominic encouraged. She nodded again, calming down her nerves as much as she could. She felt another presence enter the room and turned to see

Donnell and a young man behind him. Donnell spoke as he entered, and he and Dominic exchanged greetings, but Ashiree focused on the younger man. She took a couple of steps as he did the same. Tears misted in her eyes as he stood before her. She saw him extend his hand in greeting.

"Hi, I'm Ashden." He said. She smiled, not the least bit ashamed of the tears that slipped from her eyes as she took his hand in hers.

"Hi. I'm Ashiree, your sister."

Donnell watched with Dominic from his conference room as Ashiree and Ashden talked in the sitting room.

"Things seem to be going well." Donnell stated as Dominic leaned against his desk with his hands in his pockets. He nodded before speaking.

"I hope for Ashiree's sake, it stays that way." He said.

"Do you believe it won't?" Donnell asked.

"What I believe is that, for the last year, Ashiree has been waiting for this moment. I hope this is the start of something he plans to continue." Donnell nodded at Dominic's words.

"It hasn't been easy for him. He doesn't want his mother's feelings hurt." Donnell replied.

"I don't want my wife's feelings hurt." Dominic countered.

"There is bound to be some hurt." Donnell said. He heard Dominic take a deep breath, then stand to his full height to walk around his desk and sit in the chair.

"Where's Sean? I didn't see him when we came through the gate." Donnell asked, slightly changing the subject.

"He's with Arion at Darwin and Kelsey's." Dominic answered.

"I'm glad he's working out."

"He is. It gives me peace of mind when I'm not around either of them." Dominic admitted.

"So, you're thinking of keeping him around permanently?"

"Yes, even though I'm pretty sure the threat with Morton is over. I can't risk it. It's a different worry that comes with a family. Plus, I think Ashiree likes having Sean around. She'd never admit it to me, but I think she's still shaken up from the kidnapping."

"That's understandable."

"It is, but why do you ask?"

"I'm thinking about venturing into private security." Donnell stated.

"Because of Sean?" Dominic asked with a quirked

brow.

"Sean, Flynn, a few others. There are a lot of men that are retired or discharged from some sort of military. Regular security just seems like a slap in the face for what some of these men can do. And most don't want to go into law enforcement." Donnell answered.

"Private security is definitely more high-end." Dominic agreed.

"I think it will give them more versatility. Sean, being the exception, of course, since he would be permanently placed with you."

"How's that going to work out with the CIA?" Dominic asked. Donnell finally took a seat in the chair in front of Dominic's desk.

"I'm only supposed to be a part-time operative with the CIA. With all that's happened in the last year, I've garnered a lot of unwanted attention."

"Are you in trouble?"

"No, quite the opposite. They want me more in a full-time position."

"And that's a bad thing?" Dominic asked.

"Not bad, just not what I want anymore." Donnell admitted.

"So, private security is what you want?"

"I see a need, plus I have the resources and

connections to make it happen."

"I think that would be great for you." Dominic said, then shifted his gaze past Donnell to see Ashiree laughing at something Ashden said.

"The conversation seems to be going well between them." Donnell said as he watched the two interact. His mind ventured to another person linked to Ashiree's past. Donnell hadn't shared the information with anyone else, allowing that individual time to process the knowledge themselves. But watching Ashiree enjoy the conversation with Ashden, Donnell wondered if he should tell Dominic.

"So, how are things going with that baker Dillon mentioned?" Dominic asked, interrupting his thoughts. Donnell chuckled.

"You seem quite interested in my love life suddenly." Donnell teased.

"You haven't asked my wife for any sweets in over a month. This baker might become my new best friend." Donnell threw his head back and laughed. His little baker had finally called him, but they hadn't set up a time to go on a date. Not that he was worried, he knew exactly where to find her. Donnell understood she had a business to run, but he also wanted to explore whatever chemistry was flowing between them.

"I'm working on her." Donnell said.

Brandy was stirring and mixing rocking to the music on her playlist when Staci walked into the bakery kitchen.

"Good Morning, Staci." She called out.

"Good Morning. What's got you in such a good mood." Staci asked as she grabbed her apron and tied it around her waist. Brandy smiled, not having one particular reason for her cheery disposition.

"I don't know. I just woke up feeling very refreshed and happy." Brandy admitted.

"Did you finally call Donnell?" Staci asked.

"We talked last night." Brandy said, trying to hide her smile.

"Ah, that explains the good mood then." Staci teased.

"No, it's not just that, but it might be a part of it." She responded. She grabbed the kneaded dough for the pastries she would serve today.

"What kind of flavor are you specializing in today?" Staci asked while grabbing the items from the cabinet to set up the coffee bar.

"I am trying a coconut surprise." Staci frowned. She wasn't big on coconut.

"I guess I'll be snacking on the leftover chocolate batter." Staci grunted. Brandy laughed.

"No can do, I've already used it." Brandy said, grabbing the tray of dough and filling it to place it in the oven.

"Well, back to the interesting topic of the day, how did the phone call go? Did you guys set a date?" Staci asked.

"Not officially, but he told me we were going to date." Brandy waited until Staci caught her emphasis on the word 'tell'.

"Wait, he told you..." Staci said with air quotes before she continued. "...but didn't ask you?"

"Yes." Brandy said, resting her hip on the counter of the sink.

"And you're still talking to him?" Staci questioned.

"It was different, Staci."

"How so?" Staci asked, grabbing the variety of coffee creamers from the fridge.

"I mentioned the same thing to him, and instead of giving me some cocky, 'I'm god's gift to women' answer, he just said he didn't want to allow me the opportunity to say no."

"But you could still say no." Staci responded.

"I told him that too. He countered, saying he'd

bring in reinforcements." Brandy said, giving Staci a knowing look. She threw her head back and laughed.

"Guilty as charged, but I won't reinforce a guy who plans to control your life."

"I don't think Donnell's like that. His tone was more cautious than controlling. He has a protective side, though." Brandy added.

"What do you mean?"

"I ordered food right before he called, and you know how you put your phone down or call someone back when the food arrives?" Staci nodded. "Well, he asked me to take the phone with me to the door, claiming it was better safe than sorry." Brandy finished. Staci shrugged her shoulders.

"I'm not surprised. He's into cyber securities."

"Yes, but that's computers, not anything physical. I don't know. It was weird but in a good way. I liked it." She admitted. There was something about his concern with her safety, even with something as small as food delivery, that piqued her interest in him.

"Well, I disagree about the physical part. I can see the definition in his arms through every shirt he wears."

"Staci!"

"What? I'm married, not blind. Plus, he's taller than any other man I know. I'm sure he could hold his own."

Staci responded. Brandy nodded, thinking the same about Donnell. He was very tall, slender in build, but muscular.

"So, you've decided to let him take you on a date?" Staci asked. Brandy nodded, and the timer buzzed, indicating the pastries were ready. The conversation steered to Staci and her family while Brandy finished the rest of her treats and tarts before the bakery opened.

Donnell rested back in his chair as the waiter placed the table settings on the reserved table for him and Brandy. She hadn't arrived yet, and Donnell didn't mind waiting. He'd offered to pick her up but liked that Brandy aired on the side of caution, not immediately letting him know where she lived. Not that he couldn't find out if he wanted to but still admiring that she hadn't freely given up that information so soon. He nodded to the waiter that everything looked alright and glanced up just in time to see Brandy walking through the restaurant doors. Their table in the back allowed for some privacy. Donnell was able to watch her walk through the restaurant before Brandy made her way to the table. And man, did he like what he saw. Brandy wore a dark green, off-the-shoulder dress that hit just at her lower thigh. With her sultry curves and height, she looked like a goddess gracing the restaurant with her presence. He stood as she approached their table and took in her appearance. Her mocha brown skin radiated against the lights in the restaurant. Her locs rested on one side of her shoulders, bringing attention to the gold necklace that fell in layers over her breast.

"You look beautiful." He told her, not finding any other words to describe her.

"Thank you. You clean up nice, yourself." Brandy told him. He couldn't even remember what he put on, completely mesmerized by her. The waiter approached while they were still standing.

"Sorry." He said, quickly moving to hold out her chair.

"Thank you." She said again. Donnell helped scoot her chair up to the table before taking his own seat. He blew out a sigh and gladly accepted the menu from the waiter. Donnell needed a distraction. Seeing Brandy tonight, compared to the many times he'd seen her, hair up, apron on over a 'Branded Flavor' t-shirt, did nothing to prepare him for now.

"Can I have a minute?" she asked the waiter. He nodded and excused himself, allowing them to look over the menu further.

"How was your drive here?" Donnell asked.

"Not too bad. Traffic was surprisingly light."

Donnell quirked a brow at her words.

"What do you mean?"

"The Rockets are playing." She explained casually, looking over the menu. Donnell nodded to her reference to the basketball game going on tonight. The Mexican restaurant wasn't too far from the Toyota Center, where all the home games for the Houston Basketball team played.

"Do you like basketball?" he asked. Brandy shrugged while placing her menu down on the table.

"Not really, my dad does, though. So, I know a little about the game. What about you? Do you like basketball?" she asked. He placed his own menu down, wanting to give her his full attention.

"Yes. I like all sports, actually." He responded.

"Did you play any sports growing up?" she asked. Donnell smiled slightly, not surprised by her question. Most people associated sports with him, due to his height.

"When I was younger, mostly through high school. I played basketball and baseball, and a little bit of soccer too."

"Did you ever think of going pro?" she inquired.

"No." Donnell said, shaking his head. "I like sports but never enough to want to make a profession out of it." He continued. She nodded as the waiter returned with glasses of water, and they both placed their orders.

"So, what do you do? I read your business card, and I'm not sure what cyber security really means?" He slightly chuckled.

"Do you have Norton or McAfee installed on your computer or laptop?" he asked.

"Yes, one of those is offered by my internet company." She answered.

"Picture that, but on a much broader and more secure scale. Most of my clients are corporations, with tons of data and personal intel they want to be secured." He explained, leaving out the part of his job that tied him to the CIA.

"Do you fix computers also?" she asked.

"I can, but not so much. It is a minor service offered. The guys I hire handle most of that type of work. We have quite a few older customers that bring in hard drives after they crash, trying to retrieve documents or photos." He answered, then reached to take a sip of his water.

"So, I would call your guys if I needed something fixed on my laptop." Donnell paused the rim of the glass at his lips, taking in her words. He carefully took a drink, ensuring he didn't choke before placing the glass back on the table. His eyes never left hers.

"No, if you need anything fixed, I'm who you would call."

Chapter Seven

The heat in the restaurant turned up a few degrees, or Brandy's body was heating at the intense gaze of Donnell's eyes as he responded to her words. She wasn't even sure why she'd said them. One minute they were talking about cyber stuff that she honestly didn't understand, and the next thing she knew, she saw his hands reaching for his glass, and thoughts of his fingers moving and working on cords or wires shifted into her mind. It was a very sexy scene with him, those same fingers intertwined in her hair, working their way up and down her body.

She blinked a few times, attempting to maintain her composure. She was in a ball of nerves since the moment she arrived. The minute Donnell stood up to greet her, the butterflies in her stomach began to flutter. She couldn't help but admire him dressed in a gray button-up, black slacks, black shoes. The sleeves in his button-up were slightly pulled up his arms, and her mouth watered at the sight of his collar, resting against his neck with the top button unloosed. She smiled her best smile and ignored the moan that wanted to escape her mouth as she took in the scent of his cologne. She'd quickly taken the menu from the waiter to regain some wits about her. She pretended to look over the menu, knowing she ate the same thing when eating Mexican food, Enchiladas. Chicken, beef, shrimp, or a combo of all three, her order was the same. She just needed a distraction from staring at Donnell.

She would not be ordering a margarita tonight. Any amount of alcohol wouldn't help her constant babbling or bombarding him with questions. She thought asking him about his job or career would be safe. She hoped it would be a little boring and help simmer down her attraction to him. It didn't work, Donnell's smooth voice, the way he slightly smiled and one side of his mouth went higher than the other. His clean-shaven chin with a well-trimmed goatee made his lips look incredibly kissable.

"Brandy." She blinked, realizing he'd called her name more than once.

"Yes." She managed to answer.

"I asked if you had a computer you needed me to fix?" she shook her head no, but honestly, she would break her laptop just to have him fix it. The waiter arrived with their food, and she was given a reprieve from saying anything else at the moment. She said grace and answered the few questions Donnell asked her as they ate. As much as she loved Mexican food or food she didn't crave the items on her plate. What she craved was the six-foot-seven Adonis sitting across from her.

Donnell leaned back in his chair and rubbed his eyes after looking at his laptop for the last three hours. The current intel he'd found led him to foreign funds being sourced to a U.S. investment company already under minor investigation with the FBI. He contacted the local agent on the case and requested a meeting to go over the details and officially pass the case on to the FBI. The chime from his laptop showed an incoming email. He leaned forward and clicked his mouse to open the body of the email. The agent handling the case agreed to a meeting but couldn't discuss the details for a few weeks. Donnell scuffed *'Leave it to the FBI to put something off',* he thought. Responding, he saved the time and appointment on his calendar and leaned back into his chair again.

Thoughts of his date with Brandy now at the forefront of his mind. A slow smile appeared on his face thinking about their conversation. To say things turned up a notch at the restaurant was an understatement. The arrival of their food seem to help cool things down between them, but only a little. Donnell was a very observant man, and he'd noticed every time Brandy's eyes connected to his. The heat and fire behind those eyes made it extremely hard to keep small talk as they ate their meal. Once they finished, he walked her to her car. The November night air was cool against his face as they made their way to her car. The chemistry between them flowed hot as he opened her car door. Her short intake of breath was heard over the nightly sounds of other patrons leaving the restaurant and cars passing by. It took every ounce of control he had to lean in and press a kiss to her cheek, thanking her for a lovely evening with the hope of another date. The sweet and partially shy smile that appeared on her face confirmed there would be another date. He stood in the same spot long after watching her leave the parking lot in deep thought. Brandy did something to him. His initial infatuation with her talents in the kitchen was morphing into desire. Donnell wanted to know everything he could about her. A quick thought into doing a background check entered his mind, but he quickly dismissed it and decided he wanted Brandy to tell him everything about her in time.

His phone buzzed, bringing him back to the present. Reaching for it, he saw a reminder about

Thursday dinner at Blake Manor. Since college, each of his six closest friends ventured off into their careers. Life took them in different directions, and even though they stayed in touch, they had not gotten together very often before last year. Donnell saw Dillon the most because they were cousins. Dominic was next in line, especially after the death of his grandfather and the scandal that erupted, between Blake Enterprises and Gateway Pharmaceuticals. Then there was Dustin. A multi-billionaire now, happily secluded on his ranch outside of San Antonio. Dustin was raised in a non-popular area outside of Cancun, Mexico, and lived with his mother until he was ten. Dustin had not been aware of his fathers' wealth before that time. Preston David Shaw built a massive real-estate empire, owning countless residential and commercial properties throughout the United States. Donnell and Dustin communicated quite often. Dustin loved inventing gadgets or taking others' inventions and making them better. The last time Donnell had spoken to Dustin, he was working on a sensor that allowed detection of any device used to spy on travelers staying in Airbnb's. Donnell remembered chuckling after listening to Dustin's complete shock from watching the movie '13 Cameras' with his wife.

Donnell's interaction with Damien, Dexter, and Darwin had been the least. Damien still lived in Houston, but his baseball schedule and social life kept him occupied. Darwin and Dexter both recently moved back to Houston. Shortly after graduating from college, Darwin fled to Miami, struggling to cope with his mother's murder, while Dexter moved to California to build his Fitness empire from the ground up. Donnell had not witnessed Dexter's success, but he was proud of him.

Now they saw each other at least twice a month. Baseball season was over, and Damien was a regular at Blake Manor. Dustin made it a point to fly in at least twice a month. It was refreshing to be around them. Their lives were changing, some more quickly than others, and it felt good to be together. He hadn't realized how much he missed being around them. The constant banter between Dexter, Dillon, and Damien. The quiet sidebar conversations between Dominic and Darwin, and Donnell's techy interest dialogue with Dustin. He loved it and didn't even recognize he'd missed it until Thursday nights became a regular thing. He sent a quick text to Ashiree confirming he would be there. She responded by asking him if there were any specific desserts he wanted. Before he could replied, a text from Dominic popped up, asking him to ignore that question. Donnell shook his head and laughed, realizing he was on a group text with Dominic and Ashiree. He responded anyway, telling Ashiree he was open to any dessert she wanted to make him, which naturally prompted Dominic to text, *He has his baker to make him whatever dessert he wants*. Donnell laughed again and sent a smiley face emoji. The banter between the couple went for a couple of more texts before they must have decided to either stop texting or continue in a private text.

Donnell placed his phone back down and rotated his neck before resting back in his chair. His thoughts were replaying the banter between Dominic and Ashiree. He liked how they teased one another, challenged, and yet strengthened each other in many ways. She was his mate. No matter her background or upbringing, Ashiree was the perfect woman for Dominic. His thoughts shifted back to Brandy. He couldn't decide yet on if she were the perfect woman for him. She piqued his interest, more so than any other woman. For the first time in a long while, he considered his future and having a special someone at his side. Donnell wasn't getting younger, but at thirty-one, he wasn't old either. His parents had gotten married late in their twenties, although he hadn't been born more than a decade later. Marriage, kids, family vacations seem to occupy his thoughts more and more. It could be a direct effect of the changes in his life. Dominic and Dustin were both happily married, and now Darwin and Kelsey were engaged. He didn't see Dexter or Damien rushing down the aisle anytime soon, and Dillon, well, he was a hopeless romantic at his core. Donnell let the thought linger a little longer before he got a hold of himself and stood. Stretching, he checked the time and decided to check on the guys in the front of the store. They assured him everything was well and did a little recap on the few customers that came in. Donnell nodded, checked the calendar for any upcoming appointments, and then headed back to his office.

"**Any special** reason for the smile is on your face." Staci said, entering the bakery's kitchen. Brandy didn't even pretend like she didn't know what Staci was referring to. She was in a good mood. After chiding herself over and over for her babbling off during her date with Donnell, she finally accepted that he liked her. The chemistry flowing between them during dinner was magnetic. She thought for a few moments she was dreaming or reading the signs wrong. She hadn't. The minute Donnell took her hand, walked her to the car, and then placed the sweetest kiss on her cheek, bidding her goodnight, she knew she didn't imagine anything.

"I take it the date went well." Staci continued after

grabbing and tying her apron around her waist.

"Yes, it went better than well, Staci." She admitted.

"Oh really? Like hot sex after better?"

"Staci! I'm not having sex on the first date."

"Well, when is the second date?" Brandy looked over at her annoyingly.

"We haven't set it yet." Brandy said, putting the first batch of treats in the oven.

"I'm sorry, Bran. I'm just so horny it's ridiculous." Staci said in frustration.

"Still no action from Neil?"

"No, and I'm starting to worry." Staci admitted.

"Worry? How?" Brandy asked, focusing her attention on her friend.

"Like he might be cheating."

"Oh, Staci, you can't think that." She tried not to regret the words instantly. Brandy knew more about cheating husbands than most would assume. Staci sighed and leaned against the counter across from her.

"We've never gone this long, Brandy. It just seems like he finds every excuse not to have sex. What man does that?" Brandy didn't have an immediate answer for that. But looking at her friend in distress did something to her heart.

"Try having a date night or role-play like strangers

and end up having a one-night stand in a hotel." Staci laughed a little, and Brandy could see her nodding her head.

"So, you're saying I'm the type of girl who gives it up on the first night?" Staci teased.

"If the shoe fits." Brandy teased back, bringing a full smile to Staci's face.

"You're right." Staci admitted, then stood from the counter and walked over to Brandy. "Thanks Bran." She said, bringing her in for a hug.

"Of course." Brandy replied, accepting the hug.

"Now, let's get back to you telling me about this non-sex date you had." Staci stated while taking a step back. Brandy couldn't help but chuckle as she relived her date with Donnell with Staci.

"**Something** smells good in here, Ms. Anita." Tricia Nadia Shaw exclaimed while walking into her kitchen. She officially had a slight waddle in her walk.

"You say that every time you walk into my kitchen." Anita teased. She smiled and took her seat in the small nook area of the kitchen.

"That's because it is always true. Do you need any help?" Tricia asked.

"Not now, but I do have some pie crust. I'll need help pinching if you are up to it." Anita answered.

"I'd love to. I just hope I'm not too tired." Tricia answered. She was thrilled to be pregnant, loving every second of knowing she was carrying Dustin's child. Their road to happily ever after had a twelve-year detour, and now, she chose to savor every minute and appreciate each moment with her husband.

"I think it's perfectly natural to be tired. How about some tea?" Anita offered.

"Sure, but I can get it." Tricia stated as she started to rise from her seat.

"Nonsense, you sit right there and relax." Anita said to her sternly. Tricia's instant defiant streak almost raised its ugly head. She wasn't used to taking orders or not doing things her way. But the softer side of her, which had been Nadia Bolton for twelve years, allowed her to recognize the difference between someone wanting to control her and someone wanting to help her. She relented and sat down. Deep inside, she knew Ms. Anita felt like a mother hen. These last few weeks of being pregnant, she'd supported Tricia in ways she hadn't known she'd needed. Ms. Anita was the closest thing Tricia had to a mother. Her mother, or the only one she'd known, was awaiting sentencing for kidnapping her as a child, as well as assisting in the illegal adoption of several other children from mother's serving time in correctional facilities. The scandal made national news, and Tricia could not have been more thankful to be secluded on Dustin's land that spanned one hundred and twenty-five acres right outside the San Antonio city limits. No news reporters or media were allowed on Dustin's' land, and he'd even invented a sensor to monitor the entire area to ensure no unwanted guests stepped foot onto his property without his knowledge.

"Thank you, Ms. Anita." She finally said as Anita put the kettle on the stove to heat the water. Anita was old school and used a kettle and a teapot. When Tricia made her tea, she would use the microwave to heat some water and drop in a tea bag.

"So, have you told Dustin the news yet?" Anita inquired. Tricia smiled to herself, thinking of the news she had for her husband. Dustin begrudgingly missed the last doctor's appointment. He received a call from his grandfather in Mexico and quickly flew out to see about him. She had assured him not to worry. Her obstetrician was referred to her by her oldest friend Tanya, who gladly went with Tricia on her last visit.

"I haven't told him yet. He's so excited and nervous about one baby. I don't know how he's going to feel about two." She replied with a nervous chuckle. Her doctor confirmed two heartbeats on her last appointment. She was sure her own heart stopped with the news as she stared wide-eyed at the doctor. Tanya was ecstatic with glee while Tricia processed the information. Her doctor, at one point, worried she wasn't happy about the news and asked if she was okay. Tricia nodded as a lone tear fell from her eyes. She quickly asked the doctor if she knew the sex, and the doctor informed her they would need a little more time, but maybe by her next appointment.

The entire ride home, she'd held the ultrasound picture to her chest and prayed. Before her accident, before she'd lost her memory, she would have prayed for boys. Growing up as a tomboy herself, she wasn't sure if she could handle having daughters. Now she prayed for two of them, and she knew it was an unfair prayer. Dustin would want a boy, and she honestly would be happy to have one of each, but a very selfish part of her wished-for twin girls. She was a twin and hadn't found out until she was eighteen years old. Her twins' name had been Tara, and Tricia didn't believe her at first. The day she discovered the truth was the day she lost her sister and her memory. She wanted different for her children. Her twins. Tricia wanted two little girls to grow up together, sharing the special bond between sisters and twins that she never had the chance to experience. Tricia decided just as Tanya pulled her SUV through the gates to her home. She would name one twin Tara, after the sister she never had the opportunity to know.

"Well, I know he will be just as excited, mildly shocked but excited, nonetheless." Anita said, bringing Tricia's thoughts to the present.

"I almost told him last Thursday when we went to have dinner at Blake Manor." Tricia stated.

"Oh? What stopped you?" Anita asked as she grabbed two teacups from the cabinets.

"Ashiree and Dominic announced they are having another baby." Tricia responded. The teacups in Anita's hand slipped, crashed onto the floor, and shattered.

"Oh! Ms. Anita, let me help." Tricia said, watching Anita bend down to pick up the shattered teacup pieces.

"No, dear, stay right there. I don't want you to get a cut." Anita said. Tricia ignored her this time and was on her feet, then crouched down beside her.

"I don't want you to get cut either." She said, grabbing her hands to help her stand.

"Oh child, I will be alright." She said, trying to brush off Tricia's concern. But Tricia wasn't having it. After helping Anita stand, they carefully walked away from the shattered mess. Tricia reached in the pocket of the dress she wore and hit the button on the remote gadget Dustin had given her. Her husband loved gadgets, any type of gadget. Dustin spent his pastime creating and improving them. A few minutes later, he walked through the backdoor, letting it slam as he called her name.

"We're in here." Tricia called back.

"Are you alright?" he asked, concern etched in his voice.

"We're fine, but I need some help to clean up the mess." She watched as Dustin looked beyond them at the shattered pieces. The kettle on the stove also decided to blare at that moment. He sighed in relief.

"I'll get a broom?" he said as he walked over to the stove and removed the kettle from the burner.

Chapter Eight

Brandy thanked the hostess as she directed her to the table were her parents were awaiting. Holidays were never easy. She practically avoided them while in college. The consistent awkward dinners, and casual conversations, always kept her on edge. On the one hand, she wanted to yell and throw a tantrum at how her dad had utterly ruined everything, but then she realized she had to be an adult. She wasn't fourteen years old anymore.

"How are you, baby girl?" her father asked, accepting a menu from the waiter.

"Fine." Brandy answered dryly, slightly cringing at her father's nickname for her. She hated feeling this way, and wanted so badly to move on but was unsure of how to do it.

"That's good." her father answered. Brandy allowed a fake smile to grace her face as she glanced over the menu.

"It's nice our family could get together like this." her mother added. Brandy blew out a long-exasperated breath and flagged down a passing waiter to order a drink.

"Is that necessary, Brandy?" her mother scolded after she ordered a vodka on the rocks. *Yes, it was necessary to endure tonight,* she thought. Her father ordered a shot of Tennessee whiskey, also getting a disapproving look from her mother. He winked at her, and she almost smiled like she used to when she was little. Her mother was quirky and overbearing at times, and her father would do something to annoy her further. It was their way. The two of them against her, not in a bad way, but a father-daughter thing. Her smile instantly fell, knowing that had never been true. It had never been just the three of them. She tried not to catch the hurt in her fathers' eyes as he followed her train of thought.

"I need some kind of buffer for tonight, mom." she admitted. Her mother's face fell slightly but, she did not respond. The upscale midtown restaurant was pretty full, considering Thanksgiving was one of the biggest holidays of families gathering around the table. She saw a young couple with their two children and wondered what their story was, wondered why they weren't with family or eating a home-cooked meal. She'd had that growing up until she found out about her father's love child. After that, family dinners, holiday gatherings became tense, and awkward between them. Her father alternated holidays with her and his other daughter, which only felt like a slap in the face every time Brandy had to think about it. She received another message earlier today. Her sister again reached out to her. She ignored it. It was childish, she knew, but some insane part of her didn't want it to be real, still wishing she could go back to that day at the museum and never learn the truth.

"How's the bakery going?" her father asked, accepting a menu from the waiter.

"Doing pretty well. I landed my first corporate event." Brandy answered. Business she could talk about. No matter the personal issues between her and her father, she could admit that he'd always encouraged and supported her even when she hadn't said or done the nicest things to him.

"Congratulations. Anyone we've heard of?" her father asked proudly.

"Blake Enterprises." she replied, finally displaying a genuine smile.

"Blake Enterprises? That's a very major client to have." her father stated.

"Which event are you contracted for?" her mother asked.

"Desserts for their company Christmas Party." Brandy answered.

"Oh Brandy, that is amazing. Congratulations!" her mother praised. Brandy's smile brightened at the praise of her parents. They seemed to want to continue in the lightened mood and steered the conversation to her mother's holiday travel plans and, to Brandys' surprise, her father's nearing retirement. Their food arrived shortly, and she ate in silence, listening to her parents. It never ceased to amaze her they seemed to get along even though they divorced, and conversation flowed naturally for them. The waiter asked if they would like a dessert menu, and Brandy declined. She hardly ate dessert that she didn't prepare. Her mother promptly ordered a strawberry souffle, which shifted Brandy's thoughts to Donnell.

Her theme for last week's treats was strawberry, and Donnell visited her bakery every day, claiming he couldn't resist. He would be with his family, in what most saw, as a traditional way to spend Thanksgiving. She laughed aloud talking to him last night as Donnell told her he couldn't text because his hands were occupied picking greens. The image of Donnell picking greens wasn't one she could imagine, but he said it was his contribution to Thanksgiving dinner. His grandmother, along with his mother and aunt, did all the cooking, and every man contributed to the prepping. She loved the sentiment in that and almost sighed. She told him she admired him for helping. He laughed, telling her it was the only way he would eat. He asked about her Thanksgiving plans, and she told him she would have dinner with her parents, as usual, leaving out that they didn't do the home cooking together and were eating out at a restaurant.

After her mother finished her dessert, Brandy said goodbye to her parents and headed home. The roads were clear as she passed the city riding down I-45. Arriving at her apartment complex, Brandy parked in-front of her attached garage, watching as some of her neighbor's family members were leaving, paper plates with aluminum foil in hand, and hugs and kisses exchanged in departing. She tried not to let the melancholy moment get her down. It had been years since she'd enjoyed a holiday dinner amongst family, and she slightly envied those who still experienced it.

"**So, how** long have you and Staci been friends?" Donnell asked Brandy as they sat outside La Manderie. The weather was perfect for a December afternoon in Houston.

"Since my third year of college. We worked together before we realized we had taken a few classes together." Brandy answered.

"College friends can seem to last a lifetime, don't they?"

"It seems. Is that where you met your friends?" she asked. Donnell nodded while taking a sip of his water. He'd confirmed when they talked on the phone the other evening what Staci had said a few weeks back when she saw him and his friends at Damien's birthday bash.

"Yes, we all met in college, except Dillon, since he's my cousin." he confirmed.

"Which one was Dillon?" Donnell reminded her what Dillon looked like. "Oh, I think Neely said he owns a sports bar." Brandy added.

"Yes, Quills, it's in the Galleria area. Who's Neely?"

"That's Staci's sister-in-law. She was with us the night of the party. She has a huge crush on baseball's newest rookie." Donnell chuckled, remembering Damien's recap on the newest member of their team and the publicity around it. A waitress stopped by to make sure everything was alright with their food. Donnell said everything was okay, and Brandy ordered another drink.

"What were your friends like in college?" Brandy asked.

"Pretty much the same way they are now." Donnell said with a smirk.

"Did you have the same classes together?"

"Hardly, Me and Dustin had a few together, but I met the others during pledge week."

"You pledged with a fraternity?" Brandy questioned, surprise written on her face.

"Shocking, right? It was some crazy idea of Dillon's. He was determined to live the college experience to the fullest. Surprisingly, he didn't get expelled."

"Was he that bad?"

"No, he just tested the lines of conduct becoming a student 'a little too much' for the University's administration." Brandy tried to hide her laugh before taking a sip from her straw.

"I think it's nice, y'all pledged for a fraternity." she smiled.

"Oh, we didn't make it in." Donnell confirmed with a chuckle.

"What? Why? What happened?"

"The fraternity had it out for us from the beginning, and we just caught on late."

"What do you mean?" Brandy asked. Donnell quickly chewed the last of his sandwich before answering.

"Well, first we had a ridiculous theme?" Donnell admitted.

"What was it?"

"The seven dwarfs."

"I think you're too tall to be called a dwarf." Brandy stated. Donnell couldn't help but smile.

"That's the same thing I told them. So they let us change it to the Seven Giants, but we each had to still go by a dwarf name."

"That's sounds stupid." Brandy said.

"Most things are with pledging. However, we kind of changed it to our advantage."

"What do you mean?"

"After we were all assigned a dwarf name, the point was at random times, mainly in common public areas, one of the frat brothers would call us by our names, and we'd have to answer to it. The idea was to embarrass us. It worked a few times before we found out they never intended on letting us into the fraternity."

"Why not?"

"Plain old jealousy, I guess, or maybe to play some sick trick on us, or at least two of us?"

"Which two?" Brandy inquired.

"Dominic and Dustin. It didn't sit right with them that their families had so much money. Most of the frat brother's families were blue-collar workers, upper-middle-class, but they embodied the effort and ingenuity of the labor force."

"But what about Damien? His father is wealthy and

quite popular." Brandy asked.

"True, but Damien had to work to get into the league. His father's reputation would have got him noticed, but he had to have the talent to make it through the door."

"That's terrible." Brandy responded, and Donnell caught on to the appalling tone in her voice.

"Sometimes, our own people are our worst enemies." Donnell said sadly.

"True. So what did you guys do?"

"In his own true fashion of handling a situation, Dillon threw a party."

"What? How was that handling it?" Brandy asked.

"It was a Halloween party. Each one of us dressed up as our dwarf character. An official middle finger to the fraternity. They disqualified us after that. Which neither of us cared about. But we bonded over it and stayed in touch."

Brandy listened in complete aghast and shock over Donnell's college experience. She knew firsthand how those in her inner circle, or at least in her own race, attempted to sabotage one another.

"Well, I am glad the seven of you continued your

friendship. You don't normally see too many friendships in that large of a group remain together for so long."

"Thank you, and I feel blessed that way. But what about you? You told me about Staci. Do you have any other friends or siblings?" Donnell asked. Brandy took another sip of her drink as the waitress cleared off their plates from their table.

"No other friends, but I have a sister." she admitted, not exactly sure why she'd shared that information with him. She hadn't even told Staci. Maybe it was the constant effort from her sister to reach out to her that made her want to acknowledge it.

"Really? Are you two close?" Brandy shook her head at Donnell's question and then diverted her eyes to couples walking by and heading to and from their cars.

"A little case of sibling rivalry?" Donnell joked. Brandy looked back over at him with a half-smile.

"Not exactly. I haven't met my sister. I've only seen her once, and at that moment, I didn't know who she was." Brandy replied, recanting the event at the museum when she was younger to him, feeling slightly embarrassed but kind of relieved. It was such a burden to know, especially when she was constantly reminded of her father's unfaithfulness.

"Wow. I can't even imagine that."

"Yeah, it kind of sucks." she admitted.

"Why haven't you met her? Does she not know about you?" Donnell asked. Brandy shook her head and exhaled slowly.

"I haven't wanted to."

"Do you mind if I ask why?" Donnell questioned. She noticed the cautiousness of his voice. As if he were truly curious but also not trying to offend her. Few people asked questions out of genuine concern. Most weren't concerned about anyone else's feelings outside of their own. She appreciated that about him.

"I guess I still feel like if I ignore her, it won't be real." she answered honestly. She looked at her hands in her lap, feeling slightly ashamed hearing the actual words leave her lips. She sounded selfish, like a spoiled child. But it was how she felt.

"I think I understand." he said, causing her head to shoot back up to meet his eyes.

"You do?" Brandy said, surprised. She was half expecting disappointment in his tone when he replied to her, but all she could sense was compassion.

"Yes. It's how you cope with the information. There's no timestamp on how long it takes someone to accept a situation or face it head-on fully."

"My sister has reached out to me." she admitted

again. It felt good being able to tell him. She didn't feel the judgment or the need to defend herself.

"Have you responded?" he asked. Brandy shook her head.

"I don't know what to say."

"What do you want to say?" he asked. Brandy exhaled softly again, she didn't know, and she told him that. Silence hung between them for a while before they veered onto another topic and she mentioned the Christmas party for Blake Enterprises.

"That's a pretty big event." he stated.

"It is, and I'm very excited about it. I wondered if you might have had something to do with it since I now know you are friends with Dominic Blake." Donnell leaned back in his chair and slightly chuckled.

"Honestly, I don't know. I'm sure Dominic doesn't decide when it comes to the details of planning the company events. However, in this case, he might have." she watched Donnell narrow his eyes as if contemplating the thought.

"What do you mean?" she asked, extremely curious as to whatever thoughts were flowing through his mind. She listened and laughed as he told her of the little teasing game, he and Dominic's wife, Ashiree, like to play against Dominic. Ashiree was quite the baker as well, but not on any commercial level like she was.

"So, you've told your friends about me?" she teased. They'd only been on a handful of dates.

"My friends know a little about you, but mainly because I have a major sweet tooth. Dillon noticed, of course, and tried to give me hell about it." he answered.

"Has it worked?"

"Not at all." he said confidently, and she couldn't help but smile. She was about to say something when his phone chimed and he excused himself to answer it. Brandy did her best not to stare as he stepped off to the side and spoke in a quiet tone. It was hard not to, though. And she wasn't the only one. A table full of women close to where they were seated also appreciated his good looks. His height alone turned heads whenever they went out. She didn't mind. He seemed to be used to it and didn't have a wandering eye. She appreciated that. There was no commitment or label on what they were, which was fine with her. She just liked being the center of his attention when they were together.

"Sorry about that." he said as he sat back down but signaled for the waitress.

"Is everything alright?" she asked. Donnell seemed very alert or on edge. She wasn't sure.

"It is, but I'm afraid I have to go." he said as he paid

the waitress with cash and left a very generous tip. They quickly left the restaurant, and he escorted her to her car. Donnell leaned down, kissed her on the cheek, and promised to call her later before heading to his car.

"Dad!" Donnell called out, using his key to unlock the door to his parents' home. He heard a gurgling sound coming from the back of the house. Quickly walking through the ranch-style home, he walked on the enclosed back porch and found his father tipped over in his wheelchair.

"Oh my gosh, Dad." he exclaimed, quickly stepping over and lifting both his dad and the wheelchair upright.

"What in the world were you doing?" he almost barked,

"I was just trying to close the window." his father said. Donnell looked over at the window partly closed, ran a hand down his face, and went to shut it.

"Dad, you know better than that." Donnell stated.

"I'm not completely helpless, you know?" his father shot back. No, not helpless but limited. He knew it, and so did his father. This was occurring more, and more lately, especially on the days his mother volunteered at the church.

"Dad, we've talked about this."

"Yes, and we don't need to anymore." Milton said, rolling himself out of the enclosed porch into the house.

"You promised you would call me." Donnell said, following his father into the house.

"It was a simple window, Donnell." Milton countered, rolling into the kitchen.

"And you could have been hurt." he answered back.

"But I wasn't." Donnell stopped in the kitchen's doorway and watched his father grab a beer from the fridge.

"Dad." Donnell called his name as calmly as he could. He watched his father pop the can of beer and take a swig before looking up at him.

"Do you have any idea what those phone calls do to me? Huh? It's for emergencies, dad, not for you to make careless decisions that can get you hurt." Donnell continued.

"Who are you to tell me about careless decisions?" Milton shot back.

"The window could have waited. What if you hadn't been able to reach me? How long would you have lain there? Huh? Because I know you wouldn't have called mom?"

"But you did answer." Milton replied, rolling over to the small table in the nook area.

"But what if I hadn't?"

"Darn it, Donnell." he shouted, slamming his beer on the table, unconcerned about the content dripping out. "You have no idea what this is like for me. I'm not an invalid."

"I know, dad..." he began.

"Do you? Do any of you? I'm tired of people having to do things for me. Helping me when I eat, sleep, take a piss, shower, move from one location to another. I'm sick of it, all of it." Milton declared. Donnell ran his hand down his face again. Every few months, his father would get like this. Falling into a depression, placing him in denial of what his limitations were. Donnell walked over to the small table and took a seat. His father lifted his beer to his mouth, taking a drink, unfazed by the few droplets that ran down his hand.

"You're right, dad. I don't know how you feel. But I don't want to worry about you doing things that can hurt you either." Donnell admitted.

"I know. It just does something to a man when he can't do the simplest things, like close a window." Donnell listened to his father, unsure of the words to say. The accident changed all their lives, but his fathers the most.

Some of his manhood was taken in that accident. The inability to walk, and being confined to a wheelchair, still sprinkled salt in that wound.

"But we are here to help, dad. Whether you want it or like it. And I need you to let us."

"That's not always easy, Donnell." Milton admitted.

"I understand, but if you don't allow us, and something like this happens again, I'm telling mom." He playfully threatened, but very serious.

"Traitor." his father said teasingly with a smile. "I am sorry if I took you away from one of your cases." Milton added. Donnell had been upfront with his father about his work with the CIA. Among his friends, Dominic Dustin and Dillon knew for sure. The others may have speculated but never asked.

"I was on a date." Donnell admitted, his father's brow lifted in surprise as he smiled.

"Well, no wonder you were a little more upset with me than normal. Who is she?" Milton asked.

"Her name is Brandy, and she's a baker."

"A baker, huh? You finally found a woman to help you with that sweet tooth of yours?" Milton joked.

"Maybe?"

"Well, grab a beer and tell me all about her?" Milton suggested. Donnell nodded, then stood to grab a beer for himself and another for his father.

Chapter Nine

Brandy wiped her hands on her apron for the third time. She looked at her treats neatly prepared and properly scattered across the dessert table. The left side of the ballroom, where she and the other caterers were, included a minibar and coffee station. A few employees and guests attending the Blake Christmas Party were arriving. From Brandy's viewpoint in the room, she was able to see everyone entering the ballroom. Completely decorated in Silver and White, the lighting sparkling off the grand chandelier, cascaded tiny snow-like images on the walls and dancefloor. One side of the ballroom had tinted windows decorated with silver bells and snowflakes. The dining tables and chairs, also lined in silver with tiny Christmas trees placed in the center, took up most of the left side of the room. In contrast, the right side displayed a thirty-foot Christmas tree, Santa's sleigh, and a big red gift bag, along with the dancefloor and a photo station with digital changing Christmas theme backgrounds.

"So far, so good," she whispered to herself.

"Everything looks great." Neely said, coming to stand behind her. Staci could not help her tonight as she was helping to host the Christmas family dinner at the retirement home. Neely happily volunteered, dying to see which celebrities might make special appearances at the party. Brandy didn't want to discourage her, but she doubted Neely would get her wish. This event was not open to the public, and the only additional guests attending were those from joint ventures or acquisitions with Blake Enterprises. One particular company was Gateway Pharmaceuticals. Last week, the P.R. Manager's assistant informed her that accommodations for an additional two hundred employees were needed, explaining that the company planned to combine its company party from two separate events to one. Brandy was thankful she ordered double her regular stock or she might not have had enough to adjust.

All was going well so far that evening. Nothing was out of place, no desserts were ruined on the drive over, and surprisingly, the kitchen staff of the catering company was friendly. Brandy could recall hosting catering events with her former employer a few times, and if the same company did not cater the desserts and main courses, problems in the kitchen could arise. Luckily, all was going well. Her table was immaculately decorated to the theme in the party room, thanks to Neely. She complained about wearing the black and white serving outfit, the penguin outfit she called it, but other than that, she was a good helper. Brandy had even asked her about helping out the bakery on the weekends. Neely agreed and said now that she was on holiday break, she could help in the afternoons, leaving the mornings to her and Staci.

As more and more employees arrived, Brandy couldn't help but marvel at the formal attire worn by some of the ladies. An array of colors sparkled as they walked around the ballroom, chatting and greeting one another. Many stood talking by the minibar as they waited for drinks while others roamed around, taking in the decorations and the massive Christmas tree.

"Oh my goodness, he is so adorable." Brandy heard Neely say, she followed her eyes as Dominic and Ashiree Blake entered the ballroom. Dominic was carrying their son, fully dressed in silver and navy, complementing his father's navy-blue suit and mother's full-length silver dress.

"I'm assuming you're talking about their son." Brandy chuckled.

"I am. Look how cute he looks." Neely cooed. Little Arion was leaning his head on his father's shoulder as Dominic and Ashiree greeted employees and made their way around the ballroom.

"If I didn't know any better, Neely, I'd say you have baby fever." Brandy teased.

"It's all Cassie's fault." she admitted.

"How so?" Brandy asked, still watching other guests enter the ballroom.

"She volunteers a lot to the hospital, mainly the NICU, and I've visited a few times with her. It is so inspiring to see those babies fight to live." Brandy looked back over at Neely with a sense of admiration for her.

"I think you're right. That is inspiring." Neely glanced over at her with a smile, and then her eyes shifted and grew wide.

"Oh my gosh, he's here." she announced, trying to whisper. Brandy turned and almost laughed as Damien Storm walked into the ballroom. Luckily no one else was close to them.

"I think Cassie is right, and you seriously have a thing for ballplayers." Brandy teased.

"Whatever, I don't want Damien Storm, but he plays on the same team with Tavior." Neely explained. Brandy chuckled again until the smile on her own face dropped as the object of her own affection also walked into the ballroom.

"Isn't that your customer?" Neely asked.

"Yes." Brandy answered.

"Wow, he cleans up nice. The lighting in the club did nothing for him." Neely said. Brandy couldn't help but agree. Donnell walked quickly over to where Dominic and Damien stood, greeting others. Ashiree was standing a few feet away, talking to another lady, while holding Arion. Brandy watched Donnell finish his greeting then quickly began scanning the ballroom. The moment his eyes met hers, a slow smile appeared on his face. He excused himself from his friends and weaved his way through the dining room tables over to her.

Donnell couldn't help his smile as he made his way across the ballroom and over to Brandy.

"Good evening, Brandy."

"Good evening, Donnie." His smile brightened hearing her call him by his nickname.

"No specialized apron tonight?" He asked teasingly. He noticed she wore different aprons depending on her flavor theme at the bakery.

"No, I'm in a completely professional mood tonight." she said.

"Well, you still look beautiful." he complimented.

"Thank you." she said with a smile, and the young

lady next to her cleared her throat. "Oh, I'm sorry, Donnie, this is Neely. She graciously volunteered to help me tonight.

"Neely, it's very nice to meet you." Donnell greeted.

"I've heard so much about you." Neely said.

"Have you?" he asked, looking over to Brandy. If he didn't know any better, he'd say she blushed.

"Yes, I have." Neely continued. Donnell half-listened as the young lady continued talking, unable to take his eyes off Brandy. She looked delectable, even dressed formally in a long-sleeve white button-up shirt, an all-black tie, and a neatly pressed black apron. Her hair was pulled up into a high ponytail, light makeup grazed her cheekbones, and her soft lips held a light shine. He blinked for a moment catching on to Neely's words of compliments. She was baiting him, reeling him for a favor. He did his best not to laugh and held up his hand to pause her continued praise. He knew the ploy well.

"Who do you want an introduction with? Damien or Dexter?" he said.

"Damien Storm, if you wouldn't mind." she admitted, biting the side of her lip.

"I'll be honest with you. You're a little young for his liking."

"Ewww, what? No. I want to see if he can introduce me to Tavior Jonas." she said. Donnell shifted his gaze to Brandy, who mouthed 'sorry'.

"You want me to introduce you to Damien so he can help you meet Tavior?" he confirmed, looking back over to Neely.

"Yes." Neely said in an exasperated voice. Donnell shook his head and laughed.

"You don't have to, Donnie?" Brandy said.

"Oh, yes, I do. I think I might enjoy it."

"You will?" Neely inquired.

"Yes. This will knock Damien's ego down a notch or two. As long as it's okay with Brandy." he said. Neely gave Brandy a pleading look with a pouting lip.

"Go on." Brandy said. Neely hugged her quickly, then took off her apron, stepped around the table, and removed the hair net.

"Are you ready?" Donnell asked. He would have liked to spend most of the night with Brandy, but he knew she was working and how much tonight meant to her

"Yes." Neely confirmed, jitters and excitement radiating off her face.

"We'll be right back." Donnell said, extending his arm to Neely. Brandy mouthed a 'thank you', and he winked in response. Then escorted Neely across the ballroom. Feeling some of Neely's excitement, he held his smile in and couldn't wait to see the look on Damien's face.

"**Now, there's** a body I'd love to guard." Malcolm Flynn stated. Sean shifted his gaze to the entry of the ballroom to see Shannon Blake Walden crossing the threshold. She was dressed in a full-length sapphire blue gown. Her braids pulled up in an elegant bun, and sapphire pendant earrings hung from her ears. A matching necklace graced her neck with a sapphire diamond sitting just at the helm of her breastbone.

"You must have a death wish." Sean answered dryly, taking a drink from his glass.

"Why? Do you think Dominic would have a problem with me dating Shannon?" Sean raised an eyebrow.

"Dominic is the least of your problems if you tried to date Shannon." Malcolm frowned as he watched Shannon greet others in attendance before standing beside her cousin and his wife.

"What do you mean? She's not dating anyone." Malcolm said. Sean finished the content of his drink, handing the empty glass to a waiter passing by.

"Just because she's not dating anyone doesn't mean she doesn't belong to someone."

"Who does she belong to?" Malcolm asked, confused. Sean shook his head walking off, going back to doing his rounds. Malcolm looked back over at Shannon again, laughing at something Ashiree said. He wasn't the only man admiring her beauty. She was hard not to notice. Malcolm's eyes scanned the room before landing on another gentleman watching Shannon's interaction with her cousin and his wife, and he almost ignored it until he noticed a slight difference in the man's eyes that went beyond admiration. He blinked a few times, wondering how he'd missed it before. The longing, the desire, the need was so clear. The man's stare was interrupted by Donnell and a young woman he didn't know. Malcolm shook his head and smiled, conceding defeat. He honestly didn't have a death wish, as Sean put it. Where he may have thought to convince Dominic Blake of his interest in Shannon, there was no way he could see himself confronting a man so clearly in love with her.

"Brandy, you have a visitor." Staci called to her. Brandy placed the next batch of treats in the oven and quickly wiped her hands on a towel before leaving the kitchen. She was very excited to see Donnell and inform him of the unique flavored treats she'd chosen for the day. He mentioned his grandfather, his mother's father, used to have a blueberry patch in his backyard, and she thought it fitting to load today's' treats with them. However, the moment she exited the kitchen, she saw not Donnell but three ladies. One of them she recognized immediately. Ashiree Blake was standing at her counter, currently looking down at her son as he tasted a cake pop. Another woman was smiling and looking over at the child while the third woman looked through the display case.

"Hello, and welcome to Branded Flavors. I'm Brandy." she announced, approaching the counter. Ashiree looked up and smiled.

"Brandy, it is very nice to meet you finally. I'm Ashiree Blake. I have heard wonderful things about your bakery, and after tasting a few of your treats at the Christmas party, I just knew I had to come and visit myself. These are my friends, Kelsey Jewel and Crystal Sands." Brandy nodded and greeted the other ladies.

"So, is there anything, in particular, you wanted to taste?" Brandy asked.

"Do you have anything today with lemon in it?" Kelsey quickly asked.

"I want to try everything in this display case. They

all look so delicious. I can't decide." Crystal chimed in.

"We have an assorted mini-batch in the back. Let me go get that for you." Staci suggested, turning to head for the kitchen.

"Well, I think it's safe to say Arion likes it." Ashiree said, trying to remove the tiny stick being gnawed on by the child.

"Would you like another one for him?" Brandy asked, seeing the child getting slightly upset by the now-empty stick.

"No, if he gets any more sweets, I'll never get him to settle down." Ashiree answered.

"Kaley is the same way." Kelsey added.

"Here they are." Staci announced as she made her way back over to the counter. Kelsey and Crystal both moved to stand on the side of the counter, where Staci placed the tray of small assorted treats and gave both the ladies a toothpick.

"So…" Ashiree began, balancing her son on her hip and shifting Brandy's attention. "...do you cater birthdays for children?" she asked.

"Yes, of course." Brandy answered, suddenly nervous. Here standing in her bakery, was the wife of a billionaire. She was informally dressed, wearing a long-sleeved olive green top and a pair of fitted jeans. She stood taller than the other two ladies with her, but a couple of inches shorter than Brandy. Her slender frame belied the weight that seemed to come with having a child.

"Well, this little guy right here has a birthday coming up, and I'd like to see if you would be available to cater." Ashiree said, cooing at her son.

"I'm sure I'll be available. Do you have a theme in mind?" Brandy asked.

"Actually, no, but if it were left up to his godfather, it would be baseball." Ashiree said with a chuckle.

"Well, if you'd like. I can put together a few simulated ideas using a baseball theme, like a baseball diamond-shaped cake or little baseballs filled with various flavors hidden inside. It could help give you an idea of what I can offer, should you go with that theme or another. I can also create a separate platter for kids with food allergies or diet restrictions." Brandy offered.

"That sounds wonderful." Ashiree said.

"It sure does. I wished I'd known about your bakery eight months ago. There were so many kids at Kaley's birthday party from her school that couldn't eat any of the desserts there." Kelsey chimed in, finishing another treat.

"Let me get you ladies a business card, and your contact information." Brandy said, turning to walk over to the coffee station. She opened the drawer beneath it and grabbed a few business cards and her contact book. Returning to the counter with the book under her arm, a pen, and some business cards, she handed each lady a card. She spent the next couple of minutes jotting down ideas. Not only was Ashiree interested in her catering the birthday party, her friend Kelsey, expressed her interest in having Brandy cater her wedding. Brandy smiled as she saw the dreamy expression on Kelsey's face talking about her fiancé. A man named Darwin Knight. Staci mentioned, her mother attended his church. It took Brandy a while to make the connection. Seeing the diamond engagement ring with a yellow stone and Kelsey's mention of lemon earlier, reminded Brandy of how she had met Donnell to begin with. It seemed everything was coming full circle, and Kelsey was the customer with the 'all things lemon' order.

"Well, that was exciting." Staci said as they both watched the ladies leave the bakery.

"Yes, it was." Brandy admitted.

"You're coming on up in the world, girl." Staci cheered.

"Let's hope so. I have to do a good job first."

"Oh please, you're the best at what you do. Don't doubt yourself for one minute, and with connections like

Ashiree Blake, you're going to be the most sought-after baker in Houston." Brandy smiled at Staci's words, and the nerves bundled up again. Staci wasn't telling her anything she didn't know. But it was one thing to dream about it and an entirely different thing to live it.

Dustin Shaw rubbed his wife's slightly protruding belly. Two little miracles lie within her. Miracles, that if anyone had told him a year ago would happen, he would have been very skeptical to believe them. He leaned over to kiss her belly and looked up to her face in deep thought.

"What are you thinking about?" he asked. Tricia blinked as if not noticing she'd been lost in thought.

"I think there's something wrong with Ms. Anita." she admitted. His eyebrow deepened at her words.

"What do you mean?"

"I can't put my finger on it, but she's been quiet lately." Tricia responded. That comment piqued Dustin's concern. He'd walked in from working on the ranch or, after doing some finishing touches on a few new gadgets he was working on, finding Anita and Tricia in a conversation. Every time he'd been in Ms. Anita's presence, she was very verbal. Even before Tricia came to live with him, Ms. Anita talked with him or his foreman

Harper.

"Have you asked her about it?" Dustin questioned.

"I did." Tricia admitted. "She says nothing is wrong, and everything is fine, but Dustin, I'm worried."

"I can't have you worrying, Trixie." he said, his voice etching with unease. Tricia was still going to counseling, working through her issues of losing her memory for twelve years. Stress and worry were not good remedies to help her move forward. Add the pregnancy to the mix, and it wasn't suitable for the babies either.

"Something's wrong, Dustin." she said more firmly. He nodded, knowing when she felt strongly about a subject, there was no way she was backing down.

"We'll figure out what's wrong." Dustin affirmed. Ms. Anita was like a surrogate mom to both of them. She worked as Dustin's housekeeper for a little over three years, and he'd grown fond of her playing mother hen to him. With Tricia, the pregnancy, and even the tragedy around her mother, Ms. Anita's presence was vital to Tricia, and his wife cared about her deeply. They both did.

"I hope she's not sick again." Tricia said. Dustin considered her words. Ms. Anita originally came to his farm, seeking the experience of his horse equestrian. Like many of the patients at Maribel's, she had a rare disease for which she had not found a cure in over twenty-five years. Ms. Anita had come to the equestrian to remove another item off her bucket list. Only to find what she called her 'saving grace'. Miraculously, she healed in less than six months, and needed something more to do with her life, now that she no longer was sick. Dustin hired her to be his cook, and that arrangement worked well for both of them.

"I think if she were sick again, she would tell us." Dustin said confidently. Ms. Anita had been adamant about finding a cure for herself with all the stories she'd told him. He truly believed if she were facing health issues of that magnitude, she would inform him.

"I hope you're right." Tricia said, placing one of her hands over his that rested on her belly.

"We'll give her a few days. If you still believe something's wrong, we'll talk to her." Dustin suggested. Tricia's face brightened with a smile, and she leaned over to kiss him.

"Thank you, Dusty."

"You're welcome, Trixie."

Chapter Ten

Brandy stepped into the crowded building known as Quills Sports Bar. It was New Year's Eve, and every wall was decorated with red, white, and blue streamers. She couldn't help but smile. There was just something special about a new year. The sense of beginning and having a fresh start. Brandy looked around and spotted Donnell by the bar. Her smile grew wider. She had spent little time with him over the Christmas season. Like most normal families, he shared holidays and festive events with his family. They had been in constant communication with calls and texts. She loved hearing him talk about his cousin spiking the eggnog, an entire sweet potato pie went missing and the Christmas tree nearly toppling over into the fireplace. Her Christmas had not been as eventful. Brandy chose to spend it with Staci's family. Her most memorable moment had been stringing popcorn with Staci's children and singing Christmas carols. She'd sent Donnell a picture with her wearing a popcorn-string crown made by Staci's daughter.

Making her way through the crowd, he was leaning

over the bar speaking to a bartender. She tapped his shoulder as she approached him.

"Brandy, I'm glad you could make it." Donnell said when he turned. He instantly grabbed her for a hug and lightly kissed her forehead.

"I'm glad you're so tall. It makes it easier to spot you." She teased, pulling back slightly from his embrace but not entirely out of his arms.

"It does have its advantages. Do you want a drink?"

"Sure. A cocktail sounds good." Donnell turned, keeping one arm around her, and gave the bartender her order.

"This place is really crowded." Brandy stated aloud. People were everywhere. The mini stage for karaoke was full. The billiards area had people sitting on the pool tables versus playing. There were no chairs on the floor, and most of the tables were lined against the walls.

"This is nothing. Fight nights are the worst." Donnell confirmed while handing her a drink. She took a sip of the fruity cocktail and nodded. It was a perfect blend of juice and alcohol.

"How does your cousin manage a crowd like this?" She asked. Brandy looked around, noticing the ages ranging from young men and women in their twenties to older ones in their sixties.

"Dillon has a one-and-done rule. You mess up once, and you don't get back in. Believe it or not, most of his customers are regulars, and they appreciate and respect the rule. They are cautious about who they party with. Most want a night of good fun, but you have to be mature and responsible to enjoy Quills."

"Mature and responsible? That doesn't seem to go hand in hand at a sports bar."

"In many cases, it doesn't, but it somehow works for Dillon. He's good with people like that." Donnell answered.

"Are you saying you're not?" Brandy asked.

"Not like Dillon. I could stay behind a computer screen all day and be just as content." Brandy nodded at his words and turned as she heard a voice behind her.

"And just who do we have here?"

"Brandy, I would like you to meet my cousin Dillon. Dillon, this is Brandy."

"The infamous baker. It's a pleasure to finally meet you." Dillon extended his hand. Brandy shook it.

"It's nice to meet you too. I love your sports bar." He was pleased by her words as he released her hand.

"Thank you, but the night is still young." Dillon said.

"I'm surprised the Fire Marshall lets you hold this capacity." She replied.

"I bribe him with drinks." Dillon said with a wink, before telling her to enjoy herself and to help loosen up his cousin a bit.

"I'll see what I can do." She answered. Dillon nodded before heading through the crowd. Brandy turned to Donnell.

"He seems like a nice guy."

"He is." Donnell confirmed, looking down at Brandy. "I'm happy you came." He added.

"Staci would have killed me if I hadn't." she teased. Her statement was true, but she honestly hadn't needed any pushing tonight.

"I should probably thank her then." he said with a slow smile. His eyes staring at her seemed to penetrate her soul. The hint of teasing mixed with desire and intense longing caused her to focus more on the drink in her hand. What she really wanted to do, was lean over and kiss him. Right there in the middle of his cousin's sports bar, for everyone to see. She could not care less who saw them. Over the last two months, Donnell had been breaking down her defenses, tearing down all the walls she built around her heart, and as scary as it was, it was also exciting, intense, and riveting.

"You can thank me instead." she suggested. Her reply seemed to surprise him.

"And just how might I do that?"

"Kiss me." she boldly stated. Brandy watched Donnell's gaze switch from intense to seductive. He slowly finished the contents of his beer never taking his eyes off her. Then took her drink from her hand and placed it on the bar.

"Come with me." he said, taking the hand that was around her waist and entwining it with hers. Brandy followed as Donnell led her through the crowd, crossed the threshold hall for employees only, and opened the door to a back room.

Donnell woke with a light stretch, careful not to wake Brandy sleeping beside him. *Happy New Year,* he thought. Looking over at Brandy sleeping peacefully in his bed, brought a wide smile to his face. Last night went beyond anything he could have imagined. From the moment she found him by the bar at Quills wearing a very sexy black and silver sequin dress, he knew the night was going to be special. But he hadn't predicted how special. The minute Brandy requested he kiss her, he knew he was a goner. It took every strength in him not to maul her right there at Dillon's bar. He didn't want an audience, and there was so much more he could do with her in private.

Taking her hand and leading her to the old storage room had been an impromptu decision. The moment Donnell closed the door behind them, his mouth immediately found hers. She was ready for him. His hands and arms were kneading, groping, and bringing her body as close to his as clothes would allow. The shouting countdown of the New Year seemed to break the temporary seductive spell they were under. Donnell decided to leave Quills to take their much-needed private party back to his or her place. Brandy suggested his home, being that it was closer. He didn't argue, and they were shedding clothes before he could close the front door to his condo. He wouldn't be surprised to find a few pictures on the walls in the hallway off-centered.

Rubbing a hand down his face as he recalled the events of last night with her, he couldn't help as his smile grew wider. He wasn't a man to rush sex with a woman. His attraction to Brandy steadily increased as he continued to get to know her. One thing he liked for sure was her confidence in her body. During one of their breaks last night, she boldly walked bare through his condo, and Donnell couldn't help but admire every curve on her body. He loved the fullness of her breast, the thickness of her thighs, and seeing the plumpness of her butt, not confined by a pair of pants, nearly had him salivating. He'd explored every inch of her, delighting in how her body responded to his touch.

Donnell's phone softly hummed next to him on the bedside table, and he quickly picked it up. Checking his email, he noticed an encrypted message from the FBI agent he'd been waiting to hear from on the money laundering case Moore wanted him to look into. Finally setting up a time to meet with the agent, Donnell placed the phone back on the nightstand and put his arm around Brandy, snuggling closer into her. He knew he wouldn't fall back to sleep, but something very comforting hit him laying beside her, watching as she slept.

Brandy swayed her hips to the beat of Bruno Mars on her playlist when Staci walked into the kitchen of the bakery.

"Good Morning. Did you have a good New Year?"

"Yes, I did." she said, unable to hold back the smile on her face. Memories of her night with Donnell floated through her mind. From the minute they left Quills' and made it to his apartment, they couldn't keep their hands off of each other. They'd made love three times before finally falling asleep. That had been a first for her. Donnell had the stamina of a hundred horses. When she'd awaked to the feel of him rubbing her back and he kissing her good morning, having no concern about morning breath, she let the passion between them take over again. She was almost late opening up the bakery yesterday. The crowd was low as most people were home, probably sleeping off the new year hangover. Brandy told Staci not to bother coming in since there hadn't been many customers. Then last night, Donnell met her at her house, and they'd christen her own bed a few times.

"You are grinning like a schoolgirl over there." Staci teased and walked over to stand next to her as she dumped some chocolate chips in the batter she was stirring. "Just how good was this new year?" Staci asked. Brandy did her best to hold in her smile but couldn't and ended up chuckling. It was no use. She couldn't contain her excitement or how good she felt, more like how good Donnell made her feel.

"I had a good new year." She said, trying to sound as carefree as possible and knowing she failed at it. Staci knew it also.

"Did someone get some New Year nookie?" Staci asked, one eyebrow lifted while the other eye squinted.

"A good girl never tells." Brandy responded, leaving the bowl of batter on the counter and heading over to the cabinet to get a pan.

"Oh no, you promised." Staci asked.

"I did no such thing." Brandy answered, reaching down to grab some star-shaped cookie cutters.

"You didn't say you wouldn't either." Staci replied. Brandy stood up and looked at her as she closed the cabinet and walked over the counter where Staci was practically blocking her bowl of batter. Placing the pan and cookie-cutter on the counter, she reached past Staci and her pouting look to grab the bowl.

"Come on, Brand, at least tell me if he made your toes curl." Staci pleaded. Brandy couldn't help but laugh and shake her head before looking over at her friend. Staci was impatiently waiting for an answer. She slumped on the counter with her elbow and her head in her hand. Staci would not let this go.

"Fine, yes, he made my toes curl...among other things." she couldn't help but add.

"Ooo wee baby, I think you just blushed." Staci teased.

"Don't you have some coffee to make or something else to do?" Brandy said, hating that she knew she was blushing and couldn't keep the Cheshire cat grin off her face.

"I'll let you off the hook for now since I know we will open soon. But later, I'm getting all your secrets." Staci proclaimed before grabbing an apron and heading over to the coffee station. Brandy shook her head again. Even with Staci's probing, she couldn't keep the smile off her face.

"**The intel** you've retrieved will be a great help to the investigation." the young FBI agent said. Donnell was sitting in the Federal Bureau of Investigation building of Northwest Houston.

"Have you been able to track how the money is funneled once reaching the United States?" Donnell asked. The money smuggled into the United States was hidden between several investment firms and banking institutions. He could have dug further, but the FBI took over once the funds were found moving throughout the US.

"Yes, it seems they have been funneling between small business associations for start-up cash." That piqued Donnell's interest, but he shook it off. The case was the FBI's problem now.

"Well, if you need any more help, just let me know." Donnell stated as he stood.

"You've made quite a name for yourself, Mr. Mason." The young agent said, politely smiling, and extended his hand.

"I do what I can." Donnell replied, shaking his hand before walking out of the office. He chose to use the stairwell, trekked down two flights of stairs, and stepped out of the building. The weather was fairly warm, considering it was the first week in January. Donnell reached for his keys in his pocket and headed for the parking structure across the street. He stopped short of reaching his vehicle when he saw a black SUV blocking it. The window in the back rolled down, revealing its occupant in the back seat.

"Hello, Mason." Donnell nodded at the man. "Let's have a talk for a minute."

"I'm not sure what we have to talk about, Browns." Donnell said, folding his arms. Torrence Browns was the man Moore informed him would take his position with the CIA. Moore also told him Browns wasn't too happy about Moore insisting that Donnell be kept in place because of his discoveries in the last year. It was all a diversion to keep Donnell's clearance level high, allowing him to keep tabs on Archer.

"I think we do." Browns said with a sinister chuckle. "Hop in for a second." Donnell relented and walked over to the other side of the vehicle. The man in the passenger side, got out, and opened the back door for him as Donnell got in.

"Now, this is more suitable." Browns said, turning to face him when rolling up his window. Donnell heard the door to the vehicle lock.

"What do you want, Browns?"

"Cutting to the chase, I see. That's fine. I've been informed that you will oversee Moore's case files once he retires." Donnell didn't answer and waited for Browns to continue. The information he'd just stated wasn't a secret.

"I'm wondering why? My understanding is that you were ready to leave the CIA." Browns said. Donnell wondered what Browns' concern was, about him staying.

"Things change." Donnell plainly stated. Browns lips were tight at his answer, and then a half-smile appeared on his face.

"Look, Mason, I'm taking over Moore's department, and I need to know if I can trust the people that are working for me."

"And you believe cornering me in a parking garage would help discover that?"

"I just happened to be in the neighborhood." Browns answered, the half-smile still on his face. The CIA promoting Browns, and assigning him to replace Moore, wasn't wise in Donnell's opinion. Browns was an overachiever, craved power, and cut unnecessary corners as a field operative. They never worked the same cases and rarely crossed each other's paths, as their career goals with the CIA were different. However, Donnell never trusted Browns.

"That's quite convenient." Donnell responded.

"Look, I don't want us to get off on the wrong foot. As I said, I just want to know I can trust those I worked with."

"I think the fact that those above your paygrade seem to trust me should be enough." The half-smile on Browns' face fell slightly before returning. Donnell knew he was goading him, but he didn't care. He was pretty sure Browns had something to do with Moore's forced retirement. He was also aware Browns team was involved in the corrupted intel that messed up the Venezuela mission.

"Alright, Mason. I guess I'll just have to trust their judgment." Donnell did not respond, and Browns nodded to the man in the drivers' seat. The door unlocked, and the man from the passenger seat opened the door for Donnell.

"I look forward to working with you, Mason." Browns said as Donnell exited the vehicle. He nodded, and the black SUV left the parking garage. Donnell shook his head and finally sat in his car. He needed to talk with Moore. He needed to know everything Moore knew about Browns.

Torrence Browns shifted uncomfortably in the backseat of the SUV. He looked up at the FBI building as they drove past and dialed a number on his phone.

"Porter." the man answered. Browns gave him his credentials before asking the agent a question.

"I believe you had an operative named Mason deliver some information to one of your agents.

"Yes, sir."

"I need that information." Browns said.

"Anything specific?" Porter asked.

"All of it." Browns said before hanging up. Donnell Mason was a thorn in his side. The man was too good, practically perfect as an operative. Donnell stumbled upon a major case last year, one that had been closed by Browns' mentor and made him and his other operatives on the team look pathetic. Browns had been working on setting the perfect trap for Edward Morton, when the idiot practically fell into Donnell's lap by kidnapping Dominic Blake's wife, and failed at an attempt to take over Blake Enterprises. After the mess up in Venezuela, Browns didn't need any eyes on him or his team. Edward Morton was supposed to be his ticket to restoring some faith in his abilities in the CIA. It was a stroke of luck when the CIA decided to blame Venezuela on Moore and not Browns' team, forcing Moore out and Browns to advance. It was perfect, and he saw the light at the end of the tunnel and all the ways he could abuse his power. The one monkey wrench was Mason. Even taking Moore's place, he was informed that Mason technically wasn't under him. He was contracted with the CIA on special assignments and therefore untouchable by Browns. He was also informed that Donnell would oversee the intel and backtrack what actually happened in Venezuela. The CIA and the FBI were not happy about the outcome. That was the last thing Browns needed, but he couldn't insist on tracing the intel himself without raising suspicions. And it was clear he would not get Mason on his side. Browns was curious about the last case Moore assigned to Mason. He needed to know if any of it tracked back to Venezuela.

Chapter Eleven

"**I could get** used to this, you know?" Brandy chuckled as Donnell leaned over to kiss her cheek.

"My treats or my 'goodies'?" she inquired, snuggling into him

"Both." he answered, wrapping his arm around her. They both lay naked under the covers. The blinds covering her bedroom window showed a hint of the moonlight cascading over the wall next to her bed. The last month with Donnell was more than Brandy ever could have imagined. It seemed word had gotten around about her bakery catering the Blake Christmas party and Ashiree Blake hiring her for her son's party. Her online orders and corporate contracts tripled in the last week. She'd hired two students from the community college to help on the weekends. Neely was back in school, and Staci continued to help her in the mornings. Coming up with new treats, improving the older versions created a lot of extra treats. Donnell began visiting the bakery after closing time. One night last week, she'd asked him to sample some of the new ideas she wanted to create. He loved them, especially the ones with the chocolate surprise. Things began to heat up in her bakery kitchen, and it wasn't the desserts. Her chocolate treats were not the only thing Donnell gobbled up. After that night, their treat tasting sessions moved to either her place or his.

"I think you're getting spoiled." she teased.

"A little, and I love it." he said, snuggling into her neck. She tried not to giggle. The stubble on his jaw tickled the skin above her collar bone.

"Are you ready for your friends' wedding?" she asked, changing the subject.

"I should be asking you that. You're the one catering it." Brandy smiled at his answer. Along with doing Ashiree's son's birthday party in a couple of months, she was asked to cater the desserts for the wedding reception of Ashiree's friend Kelsey. Naturally, Kelsey wanted the main dessert to be lemon, but she also wanted to offer her guest a variety of other flavors as well. The event would be small, mainly members of the groom's church as his father would perform the ceremony. Donnell and all of his friends would also attend the nuptials.

"I'm excited. The wedding doesn't bother me as much as the guest list." Brandy admitted.

"What do you mean?" Donnell asked, lifting his

head. Her eyes adjusted to the darkness in the room and met his gaze.

"You don't have a regular circle of friends, Donnie. I mean, two of your friends are billionaires, a couple of them are celebrities, and the others, including yourself, are very successful.

"Does it make you nervous?" He asked.

"A little. So much of the new business and customers I've gained are because of your friends." She admitted.

"Are you worried about how things will turn out with us?" he asked.

"Yes and no. I mean, on one end, one has nothing to do with the other, but on the other hand...." Brandy stated nervously.

"Are you thinking about breaking up with me, Brandy?" he asked with a hint of humor in his voice.

"No, but it could be awkward if we did break up." she replied. She wouldn't lie and act as if the thought hadn't crossed her mind. She never mixed business with pleasure. If things went south with their relationship, her business could suffer.

"Don't worry. I heard from a good source that if it were up to them, you would never go out of business." Donnell said playfully.

"What do you mean?" She asked, and listened while laughing, as Donnell told her of a plot with Ashiree locking Dominic out of the colonial that sat behind Blake Manor. Brandy tried not to seem surprised, learning a three thousand square foot colonial home sat behind Blake Manor, which was just over twenty-six thousand square feet itself.

"I believe you mentioned Ashiree baking before." she replied after Donnell finished.

"It's a pastime for her, and she's pretty good, especially with brownies."

"Well, I have to admit, brownies are actually not my specialty." She said and watched Donnell's face grow serious.

"Whatever you do, don't tell Dominic that." He said. Brandy lightly chuckled but nodded in agreement.

"Have you ever attended a wedding without alcohol?" Donnell took a sip from a champagne glass containing sparkling water as Dillon approached their table and took a seat.

"You're surrounded by alcohol every day at Quills. This should be a nice change of pace." Donnell replied.

"It is, but still. When I think of a wedding, and then

the reception, open bar, and alcohol go hand in hand." Dillon responded. Donnell noticed the glass of what he was sure was papaya juice.

"We're at a church Dillon." Donnell said, stating the obvious. Dillon shrugged his shoulders next to him as they both looked across the event hall of Hope Center Community Church. Darwin and Kelsey were taking pictures with their daughter Kaley. The Photographer had just asked Bishop Joshua Knight to join, and Kaley reached her arms up, signaling she wanted to be picked up by her grandfather. He obliged, and several snaps were taken as Kaley hugged his neck, eyes tightly closed and the biggest smile Donnell had ever seen on her face. His gaze then shifted to the other side where the food table, and dessert trays were placed. Brandy stood with a slight smile on her face talking to one of the cooking staff.

"How are things going with your baker?" Dillon asked.

"Well, very well." Donnell said with a slight smirk. He recalled Brandy kicking him out of her apartment last night. Reminding him, she had to have everything perfect for the wedding. He allowed her that, but made her promise him all her undivided attention after the reception.

"Grandma Judy wants to meet her." Dillon said.

Donnell whipped his head back over to Dillon.

"How does Grandma Judy even know about her?" he said in an accusing tone. Dillon didn't even flinch as he finished the content in his flute.

"Don't blame me. Either Megan or your father are the culprits this time." Dillon answered. Donnell's first thought was to point the finger at Megan, but then he remembered his conversation with his father after his date with Brandy and knew his father couldn't hold water. Donnell shook his head and turned back to look over at Brandy. If he were honest, he didn't mind that his family knew of her. He liked her, and the more time Donnell spent with her, the more he wanted her. Brandy meeting his grandmother still seemed a bit premature, though.

Once pictures were completed, Kaley skipped away from her parents and grandfather and headed directly for baby Arion, currently sitting on his mother's lap, making a complete mess with his food. Dominic sat next to Dustin in a deep conversation while keeping a close eye on his son. Tricia sat next to Dustin but was in a conversation with a young woman at the church. Donnell noticed Damien and Shannon in the corner behind them. They seem to be in a heated discussion; Donnell wasn't surprised. Damien and Shannon were like oil and water. However, it struck him as awkward that Damien's face read more of concern than of annoyance. Shannon walked away, ending whatever conversation they were having, and took a seat next to Kaley. Damien rubbed the back of his neck before strolling over to him and Dillon and taking a seat.

"What was that about?" Dillon asked before he could.

"That's the most stubborn woman in the world." Damien said, staring at Shannon as she completely ignored him, focusing on Kaley and Arion.

"You're just now figuring that out." Dillon laughed, but Damien didn't laugh or even smirk. Something was wrong.

"I'm going to congratulate Darwin and Kelsey." Damien said abruptly, standing and walking over to the happy couple as the line of other guests extending their congratulations died down.

"I wonder what Shannon did this time to get under his skin." Dillon said.

"Who knows?" Donnell asked, placing his flute on the table in front of him and standing up.

"Are you finally going over to sample some of Brandy's treats?" Donnell didn't miss the underlining tone in Dillon's voice.

"Yes, I am. All of them." Donnell replied unashamed and couldn't help but smile as he heard Dillon belt out a laugh as he walked over to Brandy's dessert table.

Brandy didn't even try to fight the smile on her face watching as Donnell approached her table.

"Hey baby." he said, not concerned at all by anyone listening. She liked that.

"Hey yourself. You look very handsome today." Brandy complimented. She couldn't help but take a quick glance into the ceremony before setting up her table. The church staff was a little behind in getting out the tables and chairs arranged for the reception when she arrived.

"Thank you, and I like the sunflower apron you've chosen for today." Donnell said. Brandy nodded, recalling her meeting with Darwin and Kelsey a few days ago. She wasn't surprised by Kelsey's wedding colors of cream and yellow. Brandy inquired about the sunflower emblem on Kelsey's neck, and Kelsey explained how her mother loved sunflowers. Brandy's heart went out to Kelsey, learning that she had lost her mother at such a young age. She wanted to honor Kelsey's mom. It was a simple gesture in selecting her sunflower-covered apron, but when Kelsey had seen her earlier, sneaking a sample of one dessert, her eyes slightly teared.

Before she could respond, a slight gasp was heard over the room. Brandy's gaze shifted, as did Donnell's, at the person now entering the event hall. Darwin instantly stood up from the table where he and Kelsey sat.

"Oh, this isn't good." she heard Donnell say as an older couple approached the doorway, blocking and speaking with the woman.

"What's wrong? Who is that?" Brandy asked.

"That's Ciara?" He replied. *Who was Ciara?* "I'll be right back." Donnell said before heading toward the entryway. Dominic and Dillon were both there when Donnell walked over. Brandy couldn't hear what was being said, but the woman's presence wasn't desired. Brandy could slightly see her face through the men's shoulders, and she didn't look happy. Brandy looked over at Kelsey and Darwin's table as Darwin stood in front of Kelsey, who held an arm around Kaley. There were other onlookers, like herself, watching in confusion. However, Brandy realized Ashiree Blake and the people at her table were well aware. The altercation only lasted five minutes, but with the tension so high, it felt longer. The woman soon left with the older couple, whom Brandy assumed were her parents, as Donnell returned to her dessert table. Dominic went back to his table, and Dillon signaled for the DJ to play something upbeat for everyone to dance. The DJ chose the "cupid shuffle" and the air about the room shifted to a much lighter mood.

"Is everything alright?" Brandy asked the moment Donnell reached her.

"It is. Luckily her parents were here. She was adamant about talking with Darwin."

"Is she an ex-girlfriend?" Brandy asked curiously. She'd watched plenty of YouTube videos with exes popping up at weddings and receptions making a scene. Neither of which Brandy understood. If the other person moved on, then what was the point of trying to make a scene.

"Not exactly, but she acts like it." he said as they both looked over to Darwin and Kelsey's table.

"Kelsey looks worried." Brandy stated, not understanding why. It was Darwin's supposedly ex.

"I'm sure she is, but not for herself. She'll mostly be worried about how Darwin is feeling." Brandy lifted a brow at his words but decided to shrug it off. She didn't have all the facts, and now wasn't the time to discuss it.

An hour later, the entire incident seemed to be forgotten. Darwin was currently dancing with his daughter on his hip and his wife in his other arm. Donnell checked on her a few times as more guests were gearing toward desserts after dinner was served. She noticed his head nod to Darwin as he made his way back over to her.

"Darwin and Kelsey are heading to the airstrip soon." He announced. Brandy nodded, then paused.

"Airstrip?" she asked, noting that he didn't say airport.

"Yes, Dominic's plane is taking them to a remote location for their honeymoon." Donnell answered.

"Ah." she replied. Of course, a billionaire had a private plane.

"How long will it take you to wrap things up here?" he asked.

"Not long. Kelsey ordered dessert boxes for everyone to take home. I have a few items I need to drop off at the bakery, but I'm good after that.

"I need to check on my dad. Can I stop by later?" he asked.

"Yes. And I have a surprise for you." Brandy cooed.

"Oh really?" he began and crossed around the side of the table. Brandy was shocked by his boldness. As he came to stand right beside her, she naturally turned to face him. "Does this surprise include you?" he asked seductively.

"Maybe? I guess you won't know until later." she teased. A slow grin appeared on his face as he leaned down, his lips close enough to touch hers.

"I'm beginning to like your surprises." he said before slightly angling his head and kissing her cheek. She breathed in his scent slowly as he stood to his full height. "I'll see you later." he said before walking back across the room, and with Dillon in tow, he left.

"**What did** you think of the wedding?" Donnell asked Brandy. She was lying in his arms, on her bed, as Donnell slowly stroked the middle of her back.

"I didn't see much of it since I was trying to set up in the event hall, but I did get a glimpse of Kelsey before she entered the sanctuary. I like the sunflowers she added to her train." Brandy answered.

"Yes, she has a thing for yellow." Donnell replied.

"She does, but I remember her telling me how much her mom loved sunflowers. That's why I picked my sunflower apron. I wanted to honor her during her reception."

"I think that is very considerate of you." Donnell replied.

"Thank you. I heard Darwin lost his mother a few years ago." she said, shifting to look up at him.

"Yes, I can't imagine losing either of my parents. We found out about Darwin's mom right after returning from our graduation trip."

"That's so sad. I heard she was murdered."

"She was. Darwin didn't handle it well. He went completely rogue for almost six years. He came back a completely different man."

"What do you mean?"

"Darwin was pretty shy when we first met him. He transferred our sophomore year and tried to keep to himself until Dillon somehow convinced him to pledge with us." He replied.

"I remember you saying that. Do any of you still call each other by your dwarf name?"

"No, not at all. Dexter made a rule to keep it in the past once we graduated. It wasn't until Dominic got married that it even came up again. Dexter made Ashiree and her friend Chelsea promise to keep it a secret. But that didn't work for Kelsey. She is determined to guess which one of us had which name once Darwin finally told her his."

"Has she guessed yours?"

"No, but she guessed Dexter and Dillon's. It's only a matter of time. It's been fun watching her on Thursday nights, skeptically looking at us, seeing how we act, looking for clues."

"Thursday nights?" Brandy asked with a quirked

brow.

"Yes. Ashiree hosts dinner every Thursday night at Blake Manor. It gets each of us together at least once a week, which is nice considering our schedules."

"It sounds like an old-school family tradition of having Sunday dinner."

"I think in a way it is. Ashiree didn't have many traditions growing up in the foster system, and I think she and Dominic are both working on creating a certain family dynamic. One that was lost on both of them." Donnell stated.

"I remember being a little girl and going to my mee-maws' house for Sunday dinner. That seems so long ago." Brandy said with a sigh.

"Why did you stop?"

"She began showing signs of Alzheimer's, and my dad put her in a home. We hardly visited her, then a couple of years later, she died." Brandy answered, thoughts of her grandmother at the forefront of her mind. It had been those dinners as a little girl that sparked her interest in becoming a chef. Her grandmother's house always smelled of fresh-baked bread. She hadn't remembered that until now.

"Brandy?" Donnell called.

"Yes... sorry, I got lost in my thoughts." She

admitted. Donnell stroked her forehead with his thumb, and she sighed at the sweet gesture.

"I'm sorry for your loss." He said.

"It was a long time ago." She said with a mild shrug.

"You should come with me next Thursday night?" Donnell suggested.

"To Blake manor?" she asked.

"Yes." Donnell said.

"Are you sure that will be alright with Dominic and Ashiree?" she asked. Brandy didn't want to impose. She'd met and interacted with Ashiree and Kelsey in a business capacity. But attending as Donnell's guest made her slightly nervous.

"I'm sure it will be fine for Ashiree, and Dominic is all about pleasing his wife." Donnell said with a laugh.

"Is that a bad thing?" she asked.

"No, it's just different. Seeing Dominic take on being a husband and a father is pretty remarkable." Brandy smiled at his compliment of his friend.

"Well, as long as they don't mind, I'd love to come." Brandy admitted.

"Perfect." he said, leaning down to kiss her forehead. "You wouldn't have any more of those vanilla tarts from the reception, would you?" Donnell asked.

Brandy slightly chuckled.

"You really have a sweet tooth, don't you?" she teased and slowly sat up. "Come with me. I have those and a few others you might enjoy."

"Don't threaten me with a good time." Donnell replied, following her into the kitchen.

Chapter Twelve

FBI Agent Porter walked over to the employee lounge and heard snickering or maybe laughing. As he stepped into the doorway, a few of his agents were hovering over Agents Staples phone.

"I've never seen a wedding decorated in that much yellow." one of them said.

"I think it looks nice." another one replied.

"It worked out well, but take a look at this." Agent Porter watched, heading over to the coffee pot, as Agent Staples swiped his finger across his phone, neither noticing Porter's presence.

"Oh wow, those look delicious." a female agent exclaimed.

"What are we looking at?" Porter interrupted while pouring coffee into his cup.

"Staples here went to a wedding over the weekend completely decorated in yellow." one agent responded. Porter quirked a brow. He didn't have any idea what was strange about it or why it would interest someone.

"Is yellow not a good color for a wedding?" he

asked, putting two sugars in his coffee then turning to face them.

"It's just uncommon, sir." Another agent replied.

"Hmm." Porter responded while tasting his coffee. It could be a little stronger, he thought. "Mind if I have a look?" Porter asked and wasn't surprised by the shocked expressions on two of their faces. He honestly couldn't care less about the photos or any office gossip. However, his last evaluation strongly suggested that he take more effort to engage with the team. Most agents in the building did not have his seniority, but that was not considered when simply engaging around the office. Agent Staples was new to his department and almost eager to show him the pictures from his phone. He liked the kid, he honestly had potential but could be a people pleaser, and that wasn't what it took to make it in the long haul.

"Sure." Agent Staples said, walking the few steps over to where Porter stood.

"I think I'll get back to work." one of his other agents said. The other two nodded and exited the employee lounge.

"Do you like going to weddings?" Agent Porter asked Staples, taking a stab at small talk.

"I guess they're alright. I helped set up the event hall for the reception. I did not actually attend the wedding." Staples explained while showing him a few more pictures. Porter sipped his coffee, pretending interest, as Staples explained how his mother volunteered for her church and needed his help. He smirked, remembering when he was a young boy, and his mother would ask him to stack chairs and help around their church.

"Oh wow..." Staples began bringing Porter's focus back to Staples phone. "...I didn't realize he was there." Staples finished.

"Who?" Porter asked. At the same time, Staples used his two fingers to expand a corner of the picture with a man standing next to a woman behind a dessert table.

"Small world, huh?" Staples said with a shrug of his shoulders. Porter nodded and soon headed back to his office. With his coffee cup in hand, he smiled inwardly, taking a seat behind his desk. He picked up his private line and dialed a number. The phone rang twice before the line picked up.

"This better be good, Porter." Browns answered.

"I think you'll like what I've found out." Porter replied.

"Then get on with it." Browns urged. Porter smirked as he leaned back in his chair and shared the knowledge he'd just learned with Browns. After their call, he couldn't help the sense of pride he felt. *Some good came out of small talk*, he thought.

Brandy watched from her doorway as Donnell hopped into his car, after kissing her on her cheek goodnight, and driving away. The night had not gone as she'd hoped. What started with so much excitement about seeing the inside of Blake manor for the first time ended with a slight damper on everyone's mood. Closing her apartment doors as she saw Donnell's taillights leave her apartment complex, she sighed. Thursday night dinner at Blake Manor had genuinely felt like a traditional Sunday dinner. Everyone made her feel welcomed, and Brandy witnessed firsthand the special bond and banter between the group. They all gathered together in the sitting room after a mini-tour, given to her by Kelsey Jewel. Kelsey was redecorating the Manor.

The room looked more like a small library. There were built-in bookcases almost to the ceiling, a double-sided fireplace, with a large brick mantle that held one solitary picture of Dominic's parents, along with his auntie and uncle. Brandy knew of Ashiree's background but hadn't heard Dominic's. It was sad to learn he'd lost his parents at seven, his grandmother after college, and it was only eighteen months since losing his grandfather. Brandy also learned the loss of a mother, extended to Dominic's cousin Shannon and their friend Dustin. Dustin and his wife, Tricia, could not attend tonight's dinner. But the very thought of losing her own mother trickled in her mind. Her mother was overbearing at times, but Brandy couldn't imagine losing her, especially as young as some of them had been.

During dinner, Kelsey tried to lighten the mood, asking Brandy if she knew about the guy's nicknames in college. Brandy chuckled as she glanced over at Donnell. His face held an 'I told you so' look. She'd taken a sip of her drink and shook her head no. Kelsey told her she had narrowed it down to two, and Brandy listened as she explained how she'd figured out everyone's nickname. Pondering slightly on the last two names Kelsey was undecided on, Brandy guessed at Donnell's dwarf name.

"It's Dopey." Brandy said. Kelsey looked up at her with a questioning brow.

"What made you guess that one?" Kelsey asked. Brandy glanced over at Donnell, looking for any sign that her guess was correct. Looking past him, over to Dillon and then Dexter, each of their faces was blank, not showing whether she was wrong or right. A quick glance at Dominic, Darwin, and Damien across the twelve-seater table, left her with no clue.

"Well, Dopey was kind of portrayed as the silly or dorky one. Like he never took life too serious or couldn't handle a difficult situation," Brandy began to explain. "But he was the opposite. Dopey used humor to cover up how brilliant he was. If you think about it, he came up with some brilliant ideas. Although I don't believe Donnie covers anything up with humor, he is very intelligent and takes life seriously." Brandy finished.

"Is she right?" Kelsey asked, directing her focus to Donnell. Brandy turned her head to see Donnell looking at her intently before a slow smile appeared on his face.

"I guess I'm not the only smart one here." He replied.

"Oh my gosh, I can't believe it." Kelsey shouted with excitement.

"You are way too excited over this." Shannon said.

"Well, you definitely wouldn't help me." Kelsey countered. Shannon shrugged her shoulders, and dinner conversation continued, steering toward Kelsey's and Darwin's wedding and their honeymoon. Somehow the conversation shifted toward the different viewpoints of men and women regarding marriage. Dominic and Darwin's opinion favored marriage as a slight debate between Dexter and Damien countered their views.

Ashiree asked Brandy her viewpoint, politely ensuring she was a part of the conversation. Her answer seemed to shock both the men and women, but mainly Donnell.

"I'm not a typical supporter of marriage." She began. "I believe that two people can love one another and be completely committed to one another without marriage. Just like I know, two people can supposedly love one another and not be committed or stay faithful in a marriage." She finished. The quietness over the dining room lingered at her response until little Arion banged his spoon on his high chair. The conversation shifted to another topic, including the unwanted visitor at Kelsey and Darwin's wedding, but the mood had not returned to a more upbeat atmosphere. Donnell had been quiet the entire ride to her apartment. She honestly didn't know his thoughts as he had never stated his opinion, but she could see her answer bothered him.

"**Are you** sure you want to do this?"

"Yes, I need a change of pace from coffee shops. The whole college scene isn't my thing. Plus, I heard there is a lot of money in private security." Donnell rested back in his office chair as he studied Ashden's face. The young man contacted him after hearing from Sean, Ashiree's bodyguard, about private security.

"You would have some extensive training to go through." Donnell stated.

"Anything beats school at this point."

"Have you ever fired a gun?" Donnell asked.

"Only a shotgun while hunting with my dad." Ashden replied. Donnell nodded, then sat up and clicked on the information from his laptop.

"I'm going to send you a link to a training course, and then you will have to attend a five-month physical course." Donnell explained. Ashden listened attentively and asked Donnell a few more questions before thanking him and leaving. Donnell watched him go and thought more of his plans to move forward with the private security company. Sean and Malcolm were both already on board. Ashden was a couple of years younger than Sean, but he could turn into an excellent bodyguard with the proper training. Bringing on Ashden and another ex-military man, referred to him by Malcolm, Donnell decided to get the ball rolling with his legal paperwork. He had to come up with a name, a logo and register everything with the state of Texas. Donnell would also need a new office location. He tried conducting a few meetings at the computer shop, but Malcolm was talkative and a complete distraction to his workers and customers. Right now, everything was handled from his home office. But, being in his home shifted Donnell's thoughts to Brandy. She mentioned in casual conversation at dinner last week that she didn't plan to get married. Even stating she wasn't too keen on the whole idea of marriage. Donnell tried to act indifferent to her statement, but if he were honest, he was a little stunned by her viewpoint. He was traditional when it came to the family dynamic. His parents were still married and in love, having celebrated forty years of marriage last year. Donnell always believed he would follow in their footsteps at some point and hoped he'd have the same type of relationship. He'd mentioned it to Dillon, knowing Dillon caught on to his silence during the dinner conversation.

"Everything depends on what you want." Dillon had told him. "You don't have to have a traditional relationship to be happy or find true love. Plenty of couples are staying together just as long as those that are married. There are no rules. I'm sure Brandy has her reasons, and maybe you should just ask her what those are." Donnell listened as Dillon continued. "I know you more than like her. I honestly can't remember the last woman you brought around. And I don't know if Brandy is it for you. But talk to her, find out where her head is, and then go from there."

Donnell rubbed his hand down his face as the

conversation played over in his mind. He should talk to Brandy about it. But he also wanted to take Dillon's first piece of advice and decide what he really wanted.

Brandy glanced down at her phone for the third time and sighed at the private Facebook message from her sister. She had yet to decide to contact her back. The bell chimed on the front door of the bakery, and Brandy put her phone away, and she grabbed the tray of fresh pastries to put in the display case before leaving the kitchen. She saw two men standing and waiting by the register.

"Welcome to Branded Flavors. If you gentlemen give me a moment, I will be right with you." she said, quickly putting the tray in the display case to ensure she didn't drop it.

"We're looking for Brandy Pearce." the first gentleman dressed in gray said. He flashed a badge on his hip that she had not seen before and looked her dead in her eyes.

"I'm Brandy Pearce." she admitted, wondering why officers were in her bakery.

"And you own this bakery?" another gentleman asked, dressed in all black with a gun in the holster she could now see clearly.

"Yes. Has something happened?" Brandy asked.

"We're going to need you to come with us, ma'am." the man in the gray stated.

"Why? What's going on?" she said, taking a slight step away from the counter.

"Look, Ms. Pearce, we have a warrant for your arrest. We can either do this the hard way or the easy way." the man in black said.

"A warrant? I do not know what you are talking about. I haven't done anything." she pleaded.

"Last warning Ms. Pearce. Please come with us." the man in black said. She instinctively took another step back. In the blink of an eye, the man in black hopped over the counter, and she was face forward against the coffee counter.

"You have the right to remain silent...." He began.

"Wait, what did I do?" she pleaded, feeling the cold metal of the handcuffs on her wrist.

"Anything you say will...." He continued.

"Wait, wait, my shop, please wait, I can't leave it open." she continued to plea. The man in black ignored her and lifted her to stand upright. The man in gray lifted the countertop door, and she was shoved out of her bakery.

"Oh my gosh, Brandy, what happened?" Staci said,

arriving in her car and exiting before shutting the engine off.

"I don't know." Brandy cried, tears flowing from her eyes.

"Do you know her?" the man in gray asked as Staci approached.

"Yes, that is my friend, and this is her bakery." she explained, pointing to the bakery.

"Your friend is being arrested. We have a warrant."

"Arrested? On what charges?" Staci asked.

"Ma'am, we cannot disclose that information at this time. Does she have a lawyer?"

"I don't know." Staci replied as Brandy had her head tucked down to get into the back of the police cruiser.

"Staci, call my parents." Brandy yelled just as the man in black closed the door.

"I will." Brandy heard her yell back and sighed, trying not to let any more tears fall. She did not know what was going on or why she was being arrested.

"**What is** the meaning of this, Browns?" Donnell gritted through his teeth the moment he saw Browns and another agent at the police station.

"Mason! I'm glad you could come on such short notice."

"I want Brandy Pearce released right now."

"Of course, I have the sergeant working on that now. The misunderstanding has been cleared up. Besides, we can't have the girlfriend of one of our most popular operatives in jail, now can we?" Browns answered with a smirk that Donnell detested. He stood just barely reaching Donnell's shoulder as he approached him.

"I hope you will see the timeliness in handling this as a favor. One that I hope you won't mind returning in the future." Browns said in a low tone. Donnell gritted the back of his teeth to keep from speaking. He wasn't sure how Browns managed to pull it off or what he thought by having Brandy arrested.

"She's processed and will be out in a minute." the sergeant said, interrupting Donnell from agreeing to Browns' suggestion of owing him a favor in the future.

"Excellent!" Browns said with a slight cheer while stepping back. "My work here is done. Mason, I'll see you around." Donnell glared at Browns' back as he and another agent left the police station just as a couple walked in and mentioned Brandy's name at the desk.

"Mr. and Mrs. Pearce?" Donnell asked while stepping toward the couple.

"Yes." Brandy's father answered.

"I'm Donnell Mason. I've been seeing your daughter the last few months." he said, extending his hand to a very cautious Mr. Pearce. Donnell could tell by his expression, Brandy hadn't told her parents about him, or she hadn't told her father.

"Do you know what's happening? Why was she arrested?" Donnell knew the legal reason behind Brandy and a few other small business owners being arrested under fraud charges. The entire situation could have been handled with simple questioning, but Donnell knew somehow Browns was behind this and using it as leverage to get him in his pocket. Donnell needed to talk to Moore soon, but now he'd have to assure Brandy's parents she would be alright.

"The short version is the investment company that helped Brandy and a few other business owners needing start-up funds, are being indicted and now under federal investigation."

"But Brandy didn't know that. Can they do this?" Mr. Pearce asked. The answer was yes; they had the right to arrest anyone involved and question them. Should they have handled it this way? No. But Donnell had a stronger inkling; this was more to get his attention from Browns than about Brandy.

"They can, but I don't agree they should have." he answered honestly.

"Why would they?" Mrs. Pearce asked. Before he could answer, a side door opened, and Brandy walked through. Her mother quickly abandoned her place beside Brandy's father and ran to hug Brandy.

"Oh my gosh, Brandy, are you alright? Did anyone hurt you?" Mrs. Pearce asked her. Brandy's smile didn't reach her eyes as she accepted the hug from her mother and then one from her father while side-eyeing him. He slightly frowned, wanting to know why she seemed upset with him.

"I'm fine, mom. I promise. I just want to get out of here." he heard her say.

"Of course, we'll take you home." Her father stated.

"I can." Donnell offered, and the three of them turned to face him. The shock on her parents' faces did not disturb him as much as Brandy's clear annoyance on her face. She sauntered over to him.

"I don't think so." she said in a low tone.

"Why, what's wrong?" He asked. Other than her being upset about the arrest, he didn't know why she would be upset with him.

"I don't know Donnell, how about you tell me?

Huh? You didn't have anything to do with this?"

"Of course not. Why would you think that?" Donnell said, leaning down and speaking low to keep the conversation between them.

"I don't know, maybe because you like hiding things from me. Like the fact that you work for the CIA." she said through gritted teeth. Donnell stood to his full height in confusion.

"Who told you that?"

"Does it matter? You should have." she spat.

"Look, can we go somewhere else and talk about this?" Donnell quietly pleaded.

"I don't think so. I don't like secrets."

"It's not that simple, Brandy." he tried to explain. She took a step back then looked over to her parents.

"I'm ready to go." she stated to them.

"Brandy, please." She ignored him and turned to walk out of the police station. Her mother quickly followed behind her, while Brandy's father glared at him before doing the same.

Chapter Thirteen

Brandy practically slammed the door closed to her apartment and tossed her purse on the couch. She was angry, confused, embarrassed. The last ten hours had been the worst time in her life. She was arrested, actually arrested. She walked into her kitchen and grabbed a wine cooler, twisting off the top she downed it, wishing she had something a little stronger. She'd never been more scared in her life. When she had been in the holding cell, Brandy discovered that she and a few other small business owners were all being investigated because the investment company she used to fund her business was a fraud and being indicted. The police investigator informed her that anything purchased with the illegal funds would be confiscated, leaving Brandy with practically nothing of her bakery. The lease, and all her equipment, she could lose it all. She could lose everything. But knowing that Donnell had been involved shocked her the most.

An FBI agent informed her that her own boyfriend had set her up. Donnell had been the one to discover the illegal funds smuggled into the US. The money had been distributed into shell funds that looked like legitimate investment companies. Her bakery had been the last of a few small businesses that funds were discovered to be illegal. But Donnell, her Donnie, had been the lead CIA Operative on the case. Donnell had been the one that turned the case over to the FBI more than a month ago. She felt so stupid that she hadn't even known what he really did for a living. The computer intel or cyber securities company he had was a ruse, a cover-up for his involvement. She didn't want to believe he'd set her up. Or, more so, would let her take the fall without warning.

Once the shock wore off, she was angry. How could Donnell not tell her? She hated secrets, and he knew that. Brandy had been forthcoming in telling him how her father lived a completely different life, that she had a sister for almost fourteen years that she knew nothing about. How she still had issues speaking with her father and trying to forgive him when she couldn't. Not to mention she didn't even know if she was in a place to allow herself to contact her sister finally. She shared all of this with him. Why had he hidden this from her?

Tossing the bottle in the trash, she headed to her room and instantly noticed the ruffled sheets from last night. Disgusted with herself, she rushed over to snatch the sheets, covers, and pillowcases off. She tossed them in the washing machine. Even more frustrated, she noticed Donnie's shirt hanging off the side of the dresser. She walked over to pick it up, and stupidly inhaled, smelling his scent and hating herself that she missed him even when feeling embarrassed and betrayed. She angrily tossed the shirt on the floor and sat on her bed. Tears she hadn't even noticed grazed her cheeks as she thought of him. The moment she was released, she had wanted to see him, run to him, but she couldn't. He'd betrayed her, and when she'd made eye contact with him, over her mother's shoulder as she hugged her, anger took over. He looked concerned, like he cared, and he had been the one to cause this. Brandy almost caved the moment he reached out for her, wanting to talk, asking if she was alright. She wasn't, and his shock to hear her mention him being a CIA operative just further angered her.

She laid back on her sheetless bed and stared at the ceiling fan as it twirled around. How had all of this happened? What was going to become of her bakery? Would she lose it all? She didn't have any answers. But she wasn't going to sit back and lose everything she worked hard for. She'd find another investment company, preferably a legitimate one, to help save her bakery. Inhaling and exhaling slowly, she sat up, then walked into her bathroom and turned on the shower. A nice hot shower always seemed to help her think or clear her mind, and right now, she needed both.

"**Everything** was amazing, Ms. Anita." Tricia praised Anita as she loaded the last dishes in the dishwasher.

"Thank you." Anita replied.

"Not that I'm complaining, the food was excellent, but I wished you would have at least allowed me to get you some help." Dustin said, entering his kitchen and taking a seat in the nook next to Tricia.

"I told you, I don't mind." Anita stated. Tricia tried not to laugh at Anita's scolding look at Dustin, who smiled and raised his hands in surrender.

"I just don't want you to work too hard." Dustin answered.

"I appreciate that." Anita admitted. Tricia looked over at Dustin, knowing it was time to address what was bothering Anita. Tricia couldn't wait anymore.

"Ms. Anita, is something wrong?" Tricia asked, not wanting to beat around the bush anymore. She watched as Anita looked back at her and wondered if she would continue to tell her nothing was wrong when Tricia knew there was.

"I guess it's about time I told the both of you." She

relented and walked over to sit at the nook table with them. Tricia worryingly looked over at Dustin, who instantly reached for her hand.

"Whatever it is, we can handle it together." Dustin said. Tricia wasn't sure if he was reassuring her or Ms. Anita.

"I'm afraid this is something the two of you can't help me with." she said, taking a seat.

"Oh no, please don't tell me you're sick again?" Tricia asked.

"No, no, nothing like that." Anita assured her. Tricia breathed a sigh of relief.

"What is it then?" Dustin asked before she could.

"I've only recently found out myself, and I have your friend Donnell to thank for it."

"Donnie, what did he do?" Tricia asked, confusion etched in her brows.

"He solved a mystery for me that, I will admit, I truly gave up hope on." Anita admitted.

"And what mystery was that?" Dustin asked. Tricia watched as Anita sighed, and it both worried and intrigued her. She hadn't known Donnell or Anita for long, but she felt a genuine connection to both of them.

"He found my daughter." Anita answered softly.

"You have a daughter?" Tricia and Dustin asked

simultaneously. Anita nodded.

"Wait, I thought you said you and your husband couldn't have children?" Tricia recalled. Before she'd regained her memory, she'd spent some time with Anita while visiting Dustin's ranch as Nadia Bolton. Talking with Anita had been a great pastime, and one Tricia had grown fond of. Learning about her past with Dustin before she lost her memory kept her slightly uneasy around Dustin. However, her talks with Anita helped her cope more with a past life she had forgotten during that time.

"That is true. My Bruce and I did not have children. After he died, I went back to teaching as I told you before, and I engaged in a summer affair a couple of years later. I believe you kids call it a 'hookup' now." Anita admitted with a mild laugh. Tricia was speechless and looked over at Dustin, wearing the same expression as her. Blinking a few times, Tricia finally responded.

"When did Donnie tell you? How long have you known?" Ms. Anita answered her questions, and Tricia's heart ached for her.

"You've been holding on to this all this time?" Dustin asked. Anita nodded.

"Does Donnie know where she is?" Tricia asked. Anita looked over to her slowly and nodded her head again.

"Ms. Anita…" Dustin began, taking her hand with his other one. "…if you want to go find your daughter. I will help you any way I can. You know that, right?" Anita smiled at him with teary eyes.

"I'm afraid it's not that simple." she stated.

"These things are never that simple, Ms. Anita. Look at my situation." Tricia admitted.

"Did Donnie tell you anything about her?" Dustin asked. Anita answered his questions.

"Oh, Ms. Anita, you have to go and find her. I know it's scary facing your past. I was terrified when I first found out. Of course, Dustin didn't make it any better by interrupting my wedding." Tricia stated.

"There was no way I was going to let you marry another man." Dustin said.

"And I get that." she answered Dustin, then turned back to look at Anita. "But my friend Ashiree helped me. She told me she was so nervous about finding out she had a brother, finding her father…." Anita's gasp paused Tricia from speaking.

"She found her father?" Anita interrupted.

"Yes." Tricia answered. Her eyebrows hunched in confusion. Anita pulled her hand from Dustin's and slightly covered her mouth as if to stop from crying. Tricia looked over at Dustin, whose face was focused on Anita's. While her brows hunched in confusion, Dustin's perked in intrigued.

"Ms. Anita, what is your daughter's name?" Dustin asked. Tricia looked back over at Anita, whose eyes slowly met Dustin's. She removed her hand from her mouth, allowing a tear to fall from her eye as she answered him.

"I believe you know her as Ashiree Blake." Tricia couldn't help her own gasp or jaw drop at Anita's words.

Cheryl Pearce pulled into the driveway of her ex-husbands home. Turning off her engine, she noticed a man leaving the garage and getting into his car. Exiting her vehicle, she walked straight up to the open garage.

"Was that...?" She began to question.

"The man that loves our daughter." Arnold finished, knowing based on her tone what she was going to say.

"You mean the one that had her arrested?" she accused.

"No, the one who is trying to protect her from the man that had her arrested." Arnold explained.

"And you believe him?" she asked, slightly appalled. She didn't care about the misunderstanding surrounding her daughter spending a single moment in jail. Brandy being arrested was enough for her not to trust him.

"I do. Now, what do I owe the pleasure of this visit?" Cheryl chose to ignore the dry sarcasm in his tone.

"We need to talk." she stated plainly. She watched as he rubbed the last coat of shine on his car and stood to look over at her.

"About what?" he asked.

"Raven." she managed to say without croaking. He wiped his hands on a towel and tossed it to the side, eyeing her suspiciously. She wasn't surprised. She honestly never thought she would be in this position.

"Should I grab a beer or break out the good whiskey?" There was no laughter in his voice, but she slightly smiled and adjusted her purse strap on her shoulder.

"Whiskey. And I will have a glass of wine." he nodded and turned to go into the house. She exhaled, took a long breath, and followed.

Brandy saw her mother sitting in the middle of the cafe as she told the waitress she was meeting someone.

"Hi, mom!" she exclaimed, leaning down to give her mother a quick hug and kiss on the cheek.

"Brandy, sweetheart, I'm glad you could join me." her mother said cheerfully.

"So am I. Have you ordered yet?" Brandy asked, noticing a menu on the table.

"Just some tea." Cheryl replied. Brandy nodded and picked up the menu in front of her place setting. After the week she had, she was thankful to take a break finally.

"I'm thinking of getting the turkey sandwich. What about you?" Brandy stated.

"The turkey salad sandwich sounds like it is calling my name." her mother replied. They ordered accordingly when the waitress came by. Brandy accepted a glass of water with lemon.

"So, how are you holding up?" Her mother asked earnestly. Brandy wished she could say she was fine, but she wasn't. For one, she missed Donnell, but she was too frustrated with him for not telling her the other part of his job. She hated secrets, and even though she understood that he probably wouldn't be able to tell her the cases he was working on, she didn't like being blindsided.

"It could be worse." she answered her mother.

"Have you talked to him?" her mother asked. Brandy could hear the caution in her voice as if she didn't want to upset her.

"No, I haven't." she replied, looking down

absentmindedly and playing with the sugar packets on the table.

"Have you talked to...Raven?" Her mother asked softly. Brandy's head shot up at the mention of her sister's name. Her mother never brought up Raven, and she didn't think she ever heard her mother say Raven's name.

"Why would you ask me that?" Brandy said curiously. Her mother took a sip of her tea and exhaled slowly before speaking again.

"I spoke to your father." Brandy didn't respond, so she continued. "He told me Raven reached out to him about getting in contact with you. She claims you haven't responded to any of her attempts to connect." Brandy nodded. Everything her father heard from her sister was true. It was hard to acknowledge that she had a sister, but she was more concerned about her mother having this conversation with her.

"I'm surprised you're bringing it up." Brandy replied. From her understanding, her mother never wanted her to know Raven. And in some ways, Brandy felt she would be betraying her mother by accepting her sister.

"Your father and I talked some...about what happened." her mother replied. Brandy's brow lifted in curiosity. What happened was her father cheated on her mother and hid another family entirely.

"What's to explain, mom?" she asked.

"Your father believes I should tell you the truth." Cheryl stated.

"What truth?" Brandy asked curiously. The waitress brought their food before her mother could answer her question. They thanked the waitress, said grace, and just as Brandy was taking a bite, her mother spoke.

"I knew about Raven." her mother admitted. Brandy paused mid-bite and stared at her mother.

"Before the museum?" Brandy asked. Her mother nodded, and Brandy placed her sandwich back on her plate and wiped her hands with a napkin. Her appetite momentarily gone. She sat back in her chair and folded her arms.

"When did you find out?" Brandy asked.

"Before you were born." she answered slowly.

"I don't understand." Brandy admitted. She always believed her mother was shocked by the knowledge of her father having a child outside of their marriage. Her mother acted hurt and betrayed. She watched as her mother inhaled and exhaled slowly.

"It's a long story, Brandy, and pretty complicated." her mother replied, stalling.

"Tell me anyway." she said, her voice a little stronger than she intended.

"I never wanted to get married." her mother began, and Brandy listened for the next hour as her mother explained a dynamic in her parent's relationship that she never knew of.

Donnell punched in the security code that allowed him to access the top floor. Once the elevator doors opened, he walked over to the second door on the right and knocked. A few seconds later, the door opened.

"Donnie, come on in." Dominic said, stepping back to allow Donnell into his condo.

"Thanks, Dom." Donnell said, crossing the threshold. He immediately noticed Dustin sitting on one of the bar stools at the kitchen island. Donnell removed his coat and placed it across another bar stool before taking a seat.

"Do you want something to drink, or should we get right down to business?" Dominic asked.

"A bottle of water is fine." Donnell replied.

"This must be pretty serious if you didn't want us to meet at the Manor." Dustin said.

"The less who know about this, the better." Donnell replied.

"Meaning this is about Brandy, and you don't want the other women to know." Dominic stated while handing him a bottle of water. Donnell smirked at his comment. The growing friendship between Brandy and his friends' wives prompted this meeting being private.

"Yes. I need your help, the both of yours." Donnell began. He explained the situation around Brandy's financing for the bakery. Right now, she was in potential danger of losing her bakery.

"How much money are we talking about here?" Dominic asked.

"Close to fifty thousand. That with the loan amount and some of her personal money invested." Donnell answered. Dominic nodded, and Donnell could see the wheels in Dominic's head churning. Risk Management, especially with small businesses, was what Dominic was good at.

"What do you need my help with?" Dustin asked.

"Part of her lease is wrapped up in her loan for the space she is renting out." Donnell explained.

"So, you want me to find her a new location?" Dustin asked.

"If necessary, Yes." Donnell said.

"Have you spoken to her?" Dominic asked.

"No." Donnell answered. He'd attempted to reach

out to Brandy. But she hadn't responded to any of his calls or texts.

"This is a lot to go through for a woman you're not too sure you'll have a future with." Dustin commented.

"This coming from a man that built an entire equestrian for a woman he thought was dead." Donnell replied. Dustin stared at him for a second before a slow smile appeared, and he nodded.

"Point made." Dustin agreed.

"You care about her." Dominic stated, more than asked.

"Yes, and I feel partly responsible." Donnell admitted, then further explained to the questioning stare from both Dustin and Dominic.

"I'll crunch a few numbers and get back to you." Dominic said.

"And I'll look at it and see if I have a few options, but it might be easier to buy the strip mall she's in." Dustin added. Donnell nodded and tried to hide his chuckle. Only Dustin could talk about buying a strip mall like it was as simple as buying a tie.

"Well, I need to get back to the Manor and tend to my pregnant wife." Dominic said.

"So do I. Give me a minute to talk to Donnie." Dustin asked. Dominic's eyes shifted curiously between the two of them before nodding and telling Dustin he'd meet him in the parking garage.

"What did you need to talk about?" Donnell asked once Dominic left the condo.

"We're bringing Ms. Anita to the Manor for Arion's birthday party." Dustin stated. Donnell knew instantly why Dustin was giving him a heads up.

"Has she talked to Ashiree yet?"

"No, and I haven't told Dom, which doesn't sit well with me." Dustin added.

"Me either, but it is not my story to tell."

"That's the same thing Tricia says." Dustin replied, rubbing his hand behind his head.

"Ashden came to see Ashiree a couple of months back." Donnell said.

"Her brother?" Dustin asked. Donnell nodded. "How did that go?"

"Pretty good. He still keeps in contact with her, which for his sake, I hope he continues." At Dustin's lifted brow, Donnell explained Dominic's concern of Ashiree being hurt if the relationship with Ashden didn't go as she planned.

"I don't think Ms. Anita has any plans of not being in Ashiree's life once the word is out." Dustin said.

"Let's just hope it all goes well." Donnell stated.

Dustin nodded and then stood.

"Yes, lets." he responded, heading to the door of the condo. Donnell grabbed his jacket and followed him, locking the door as they left.

Chapter Fourteen

Brandy pulled slowly into her fathers' driveway and parked her car. The weather outside looked gloomy, and she wouldn't be surprised if storm clouds began to form shortly. Grabbing her purse, she exited her vehicle and walked up the short walkway to her fathers' door. Ringing the doorbell, she waited for him to answer.

"Hey, baby girl." he said as he opened the door and allowed her to step through the threshold. "What do I owe the pleasure of this visit?" he asked, closing the door and bringing her in for a slight hug. Brandy tried not to notice the uncomfortable stance of her father. He was always nice and sweet to her, despite her acting like a spoiled brat and being very standoffish toward him the last few years. After speaking with their mother, Brandy knew she had not been fair to her father.

"Hey, daddy. I came by because I think it's time we talked." He nodded and led her over to the sofa to sit.

"Your mother told me she talked to you." he said. Brandy shifted to get comfortable on the sofa facing him and nodded as he sat in the recliner next to her.

"She did, and I'm sorry I blamed you." Brandy said honestly.

"You have nothing to apologize for, Brandy. It was between your mother and me."

"I know that, but I blamed you for everything. Mom played her part, acting as though she hadn't been aware of...my sister." Brandy replied.

"She wants to get to know you; you know that, right?" her dad said.

"I do." Brandy admitted and then exhaled a slow breath. "I don't know if I can, daddy. I kind of blamed her too, for how our family was torn apart. It's been hard accepting the truth, and to be honest, I'm a little embarrassed now."

"Why?" Arnold asked.

"Because no matter what the situation was between you and mom and then you and Raven's mom. I should have been open to getting to know her. I guess I never thought about how she would feel in this situation. She is probably just as affected as me, and I blamed her for way too long.

"It is never too late to start over, Brandy. I know this hasn't been easy for you. It hasn't been easy for her either. But as long as we have breath in our bodies, we have a chance each day, sometimes in each minute, to make a decision to start over." her father said.

"I know nothing about being a sister." Brandy admitted, with a slight smile, feeling somewhat hopeful about connecting with her sister. Her father smiled back at her.

"How about working on being a friend first?" He suggested. She nodded again, taking in his words and considering that approach. It seemed more straightforward.

"I think that might help." she admitted.

"Good. Try that and see how it works out. I know Raven has been trying to reach you."

"She has, and it's time I responded."

"Great, then maybe once you start letting your sister in, you can forgive that boyfriend of yours." Arnold suggested.

"Donnie?" Brandy asked with a quirked brow.

"Do you have another young man lurking about that I don't know of?" her father asked. Brandy shook her head. "Then, yes, Donnie."

"You've talked to him?"

"He came to speak with me the other day. I have to admit I was a little skeptical about him just showing up. But he wanted to clear up any misunderstandings about what happened with the FBI and police. He seems to be a very smart man." her father stated.

"He is." Brandy agreed. She didn't want to think about Donnie or think of his betrayal. If she could still call it that. After talking with her mother and seeing how completely wrong she'd been about her parents' marriage, she wondered if maybe she was wrong believing Donnie's involvement in her being arrested. Her father seemed convinced he was working on her behalf to fix the situation. Maybe her father was right. She needed to talk to him, and allow him to explain. Their conversation steered to her father enjoying his retirement and his latest obsession with watching TicTok videos. Brandy smiled and laughed more with her father than she had in years. She was feeling slightly guilty about the time she'd wasted being angry and hurt but quickly dismissed it. Brandy was starting over, and she knew making up with her father had been a significant step, but she also knew she would make this decision a couple of times more in her life.

"**I don't know** what Browns is really up to." Moore said. Donnell sat on his back porch. The fire pit reflected well against the Houston night sky.

"I can't prove it yet, but I know he was somehow

behind Brandy's arrest." Donnell replied.

"He doesn't like not being in control. And with you overseeing my caseload, he might feel threatened."

"I think it's more than that. I'm missing something. I know I am. Browns wants me in his pocket. He wants me owing him a favor."

"Again, he wants power and control." Moore said, taking a swig from his beer.

"This is a nice mess you're leaving me with, Moore." Donnell said.

"Nothing is as it seems, Mason." Moore replied.

"Do you care to elaborate?"

"In time. Nothing stays hidden in the dark forever. Whatever Browns' reasons are for wanting you in his pocket will surface at some point."

"Why do I still get the feeling you know more than what you are telling me?" Donnell heard Moore chuckle at his response but didn't answer him immediately.

"How are things going with the private security detail?" Moore asked. Donnell arched a brow at Moore's abrupt change of topic.

"Going well so far. I have a new recruit."

"Anyone, I know?" Moore inquired. Donnell shook his head. They stayed in silence for a moment before Moore spoke again.

"You're a good man, Mason. Don't go down the rabbit hole with Browns."

"So, you know more than you are leading on to?"

"I know Browns will eventually slip up. Men like him always do. He knows you. He'll try to throw you for a loop. Knowing you're itching to solve things." Moore said, looking over at him before continuing. "Whatever he wants, look more on the surface. Don't get caught in clues you think Browns might hint at. Look in the direction he is not steering you. That's where you'll find your answer."

"And you don't have a clue what that is?" Donnell asked.

"I hadn't been paying attention to Browns over the last two years. But I will mention that he seemed quite upset about the arrest at LAX. I didn't give it a second thought at the time, but maybe you could start there." Moore suggested. Donnell thought of the arrest of Edward Morton. The man was responsible for kidnapping Ashiree and attempting to take over Blake Enterprises. If Moore believed Browns was involved, Donnell would start his search there.

"Thanks, Moore."

"Anytime, Mason."

Brandy decided to bite the bullet. She'd avoided dealing with any of her bills or creditors. She knew she needed to contact them, potentially ask for an extension or possibly renegotiate the equipment rental agreements. The first call she made was to her landlord about her lease. She left a message and decided to check on the others while waiting to hear from them. She logged into her utility app and was surprised to see her balance was zero, frowning, she looked through the previous bill and saw no charges due. A payment was made just a few days ago. That had to be a mistake. She huffed out a breath, knowing some clerk probably applied someone else's payment to her account. She'd make a mental note of it. When the utility company realized the mistake, they would send her a bill for double. She'd cross that line when she came to it. However, the utility company wasn't the only bill with a zero balance. The water bill, the phone bill, the advertising company she used for her ads. The most bizarre thing was her contract with an equipment rental company. Not only was her equipment contract paid to date, but the purchase agreement option was also paid with the lifetime warranty. Now she was nervous. What was going on? Her first thought had been her parents, but she quickly dismissed it. They loved her and may have paid a few months in advance to help her get back on her feet, but only if she asked. Staci crossed her mind, but Brandy dismissed that idea too. Staci and her husband made decent money, but not that decent. An odd thought entered her mind. Donnell? No, he wouldn't do that, would he? Resting back in her chair, she closed her eyes. She hadn't allowed herself to think about him. She fought every thought or memory that tried to inhabit her brain. As much as she wanted to banish thoughts of him permanently, she couldn't. He had been different. He was unlike any man she'd ever known, and she'd fallen for him. She loved his smile and his laugh. The way he looked at her like she was just as delicious as the treats she made. Her phone chirped to announce an incoming call.

"Hello...this is she...yes, I did call and wanted to discuss the terms of my lease...I can be there in fifteen minutes...yes, I know where that is...thank you so much." Brandy disconnected the call, feeling as though the secretary was a little too happy to set up her appointment for lease negotiations, but maybe she was just naturally cheerful. Brandy grabbed her jacket and left her apartment.

"**Why do you** look nervous like you're about to propose or something?" Donnell heard Dillon ask, breaking his thoughts as he watched Brandy setting up the party table for Arion's birthday party.

"What?" he asked, confused.

"I'm looking at you watch Brandy like you're nervous or something." Dillon answered. The truth was he was nervous. He hadn't spoken to Brandy and, although he knew she would cater Arion's party, he didn't know how Brandy would feel about seeing him. The last couple of weeks were filled with finding out how to fix the fraud and embezzlement charges against her and the other business owners. The investment company had done an interesting job in the small print of the loan documents, deeming every patron who received a loan fully responsible for the money received and its origins. There had been no way for any of the loan recipients to think the source of the funds would fall back on them and could lead to criminal charges. Over twenty small businesses, including Brandy's, were being held liable. A civil suit against the Houston FBI office was currently in the making due to how the charges were being executed. None of the patrons had a stake in the investment company. Being held legally responsible for the origins of the funds were grounds for an investigation, but not arrests, warrants, or charges. Donnell knew Browns and an FBI agent named Porter were behind it. He knew Browns was aware the charges wouldn't stick, and that the FBI would catch backlash for authorizing such an occurrence. Browns was throwing Porter under the bus, making Donnell wonder what Browns was trying to cover up.

"We haven't talked since the arrest, but I'm not letting her leave today without us talking." he finally said to Dillon.

"Well, by the looks of it, she seems to feel the same way since she's trying so hard not to get noticed sneaking glances at you." Dillon replied, and Donnell looked over at Brandy again to see her shift her eyes away and focus back on the party table. Donnell smiled inwardly, taking that as a good sign. He wasn't privy to exactly what Porter had told her, but Donnell could guess somehow Porter made it seem as if he'd set the whole thing up. The truth behind everything happening with Porter and Browns, Donnell would discover soon enough. There was no way he was letting it go or allowing either of them to get away with it.

"What is going on with them?" Dillon asked, cutting into Donnell's thoughts again. He looked down at Dillon and then followed his gaze. Damien and Shannon were in a very heated discussion. Donnell shrugged his shoulders.

"What do you mean? They're always mad at each other." Donnell replied.

"No, this is different." Dillon said. Donnell looked harder at the two of them, still bickering, and shook his head. He didn't see a difference. It appeared normal as far as he was concerned. He looked back over to the party table, and this time his eyes connected with Brandy, and she didn't look away. The sides of her mouth went up in a half-smile, and Donnell's heart lifted. He sent her a wink, and her half-smile turned into a full one before he saw her turn and head toward the kitchen. They were definitely talking after the party.

Brandy handed the last party favor to a family that lived not too far from the Blake Manor. The original setup of the party had been planned on the deck, but as April Showers began to fall like thundering waterfalls, they all had to adjust. She instantly noticed Donnell the moment he arrived. She needed to talk with him. He deserved his chance to explain whatever happened, and she knew that regardless of how it happened, she wanted to trust him, to be with him. She missed him. Her father believed he wasn't involved, and even Staci felt some misunderstanding was going on, suggesting Brandy talk to him and find out. She honestly wasn't sure if he would want to speak with her. Brandy hadn't been receptive to any of his texts or calls the last couple of weeks. She had been trying to work things out in her head, and she also wanted to break the barrier in contacting her sister. Brandy was happy that she had, and even discovered she had a nephew. Now it was time to patch things up with Donnell. When she'd been caught the last time sneaking glances his way, she decided not to hide it and just allowed his gaze to connect with hers. The moment she saw him wink, she hoped that they could sort things out.

"You didn't plan on leaving before speaking to me, did you?" she was slightly startled by Donnell's voice. She hadn't heard him approaching.

"No I was hoping we could talk." she admitted.

"I think we should." he replied with a smile.

"Can you give me a minute? I need to make sure everything is okay, and Ashiree doesn't need anything else." Brandy said.

"Sure, I'll wait for you right here." She nodded and walked over to the sitting area where Ashiree was speaking to her friend from Boston. Brandy believed her name was Chelsea. The two of them were laughing as Ashiree held Chelsea's son and Chelsea held the birthday boy. Ashiree assured her everything was fine and thanked her for all she'd done, including moving everything inside because of the rain. It worked out better considering they'd held the party in the game room of Blake Manor, which looked very similar to the inside of a Dave-n-Busters.

She made her way back over to Donnell, saying his goodbyes and speaking to a very nervous older lady. Brandy remembered her arriving earlier by helicopter with Donnell's friends, Dustin and Tricia Shaw. Brandy vaguely recalled them being in the VIP section of the club for Damien's birthday. Donnell smiled the moment she approached and looked back down at the woman.

"Don't worry about it. This is what you've waited a long time for." Donnell said. The older woman nodded.

"I truly appreciate all that you've done." the older woman said.

"Think nothing of it. I'm happy I was able to discover it. Even if it was by accident." Donnell teased, and the older woman smiled.

"I'm sorry, who is this?" the older woman said, finally taking notice of Brandy.

"Ms. Anita, this is Brandy. Brandy, this is Anita Campbell." Donnell introduced them.

"It's nice to meet you." Brandy said, extending her hand.

"You also, my dear." she said, taking her hand. Brandy saw a slightly waddling Tricia Shaw heading their way.

"Hi Donnie, Brandy." she said in greeting, then placed her arms around Anita's shoulder. "Dominic has arranged for you to talk with Ashiree after everyone leaves. Are you alright with that?" Tricia asked Anita. Brandy watched as Anita slowly and uncomfortably nodded her head. She lifted a brow, wondering what Anita needed to speak with Ashiree about.

"Dominic knows?" Donnell asked Tricia.

"Dustin felt the need to tell him." Tricia answered, and Brandy did a quick glance over to see Dustin speaking to Dominic while Dominic looked over at his wife, laughing and talking with her best friend.

"It's probably best. We don't need the both of them shocked at the same time." Donnell replied.

"True. That's what Dustin thought too." Tricia said. Brandy looked back over at Donnell as she felt him slightly shift beside her.

"Do you want me to stay?" she heard him ask Anita. Now she was really curious as to what was going on.

"No. I need to do this. And I have Nadia here to help me." she answered. Brandy's eyebrows deepened. *Who was Nadia?* Tricia playfully laughed at Brandy's expression before answering her.

"Nadia was my name before I regained my

memory." she replied.

"What? You lost your memory?" Brandy asked, surprised.

"Yes, it's a pretty long story." she answered.

"And I haven't gotten used to calling her Tricia yet." Anita admitted.

"It's fine. Technically, Nadia is my middle name now, so I don't mind." she said, addressing Anita, then looked back at Brandy. "But maybe the next time I see you, I can share that story with you." she offered.

"I think it would be interesting to hear." Brandy admitted.

"It truly is. I should consider writing a book." Tricia teased. Brandy laughed, and so did Donnell. Even Anita chuckled a little, and Brandy was happy to see some ease in the woman's face. Whatever she needed to speak with Ashiree about seemed to weigh heavy on her.

"Well, we're going to get out of here." Donnell announced. He leaned down to hug Anita. "You call me if you need anything, okay?" Anita agreed as he released her from their hug. Brandy watched as Anita walked over to where Dustin and Dominic stood.

"Is everything alright?" Brandy asked.

"Everything will be fine, or at least I hope it will be." he said. Brandy looked up into his eyes and knew the last part of his words was referring to them.

"I hope it will be too." she answered with a half-smile.

"Where do you want to talk, your place or mine?" he asked.

"I have to drop a few items back off at the bakery, and then we can go to my place." she suggested.

"Okay, I'll follow you." He replied, escorting her out of the Manor and to her car.

Chapter Fifteen

Donnell closed the door as he walked into Brandy's apartment. His mind had been on Anita and the situation with Ashiree while driving over to Brandy's place. But now, he needed to focus on patching up his relationship with Brandy.

"Would you like something to drink?" she offered, kicking off her shoes, tossing her purse on the loveseat, and heading to the kitchen.

"Sure, whatever you have is fine." he answered, loving the way she seemed utterly unbothered, discarding her shoes and ignoring wherever they landed.

"I was thinking we could talk on the balcony." she said, grabbing two glasses of wine from the cabinet as he watched from the entryway of her kitchen.

"Sure." he said, turning to walk past the dining table and opening the sliding door. Brandy stepped onto the balcony with the wine glasses, placed the wine glasses on a small wicker table in front of a two-seater settee, and sat.

"This is nice." he admitted, closing the balcony door and taking a seat, then looking out over the balcony to the pond. The sun still sat high in the sky but hid behind a few clouds. The rain had come and gone, or maybe on her side of town, the rain hadn't fallen. Houston weather was crazy like that. Blake Manor was located slightly northwest of Houston, while Brandy's apartment was southeast and closer to the Nasa Space Center.

"So, why didn't you tell me you're in the CIA?" Brandy asked. Donnell looked over at her as her eyes were still focused on the pond. He slowly exhaled.

"Only a handful of people know that information." he answered. It wasn't something he usually disclosed.

"Do you not trust me?" she asked.

"No, Brandy, it's not that. My mother doesn't even know." he answered. It was safer that way, especially with some cases he'd been assigned to in his rookie years.

"Does anyone in your family know?"

"My father and Dillon."

"You don't think your father told your mother?"

"No, my grandfather was in the military and had friends in special forces. He knows the dangers knowledge like that can have." he answered. Watching her slowly nod her head.

"Do any of your friends know?"

~ 235 ~

"Dustin and Dominic. The others probably speculate, but they've never asked."

"So, what you do for the CIA is dangerous?" she asked.

"It can be. In the beginning, I handled some pretty nasty cases."

"Were you trying to protect me?"

"Honestly, before I met you, I was planning on quitting." he admitted. She finally looked over at him.

"Why?"

"I want more, I guess. When I first took on the job, it was about the money. Gathering intel for six figures wasn't something I could turn down at the time. My family needed the money, and I was good at getting intel without leaving a trace." He watched her expressions as he told her all about his father's accident, the lengthy legal case they had to fight against the car driver that paralyzed his dad. Donnell explained how his mother's retirement wasn't enough to cover the medical bills and care for his father while they waited for the settlement. He'd spent the first eighteen months of his career with the CIA, giving his family money. Once the settlement came in, he took on more of a part-time role with the CIA, handling their more difficult intel cases, while starting his own cyber security company. Donnell also added how he was working to start his own private security company. Once he finished explaining the last eight years of his life up to meeting her, she leaned forward to grab a glass of wine and took a few sips before speaking.

"I hate secrets, Donnie." she said. He exhaled slowly, thinking for a moment that everything he'd explained was for nothing. "My mother knew about my sister." she added. Donnell's brow lifted at her words.

"Before the museum trip?" he asked. She nodded slowly and took another sip from her glass.

"Yes." Brandy answered.

"Wow." Donnell thought out loud and reached for his own glass of wine. "How did you find out?"

"My mother told me. She found out my sister was trying to reach me. And I think she was trying to help me not blow things with you." That comment made him chuckle a little. "She said things are not always as they seem. I thought at first it was just her intruding in my love life since she liked none of the boys I went out with in college." Brandy admitted.

"I guess I should be flattered."

"Yes, both of my parents like you, which is something to be said about you,

but I didn't want to hear that a couple of weeks ago." she added.

"I'm sure you didn't." he teased.

"Anyway, she told me about the arrangement she and my father had regarding his other family. It's crazy even to think my mother could suggest such a thing, but as long as public appearance was maintained, she honestly didn't care."

"So, she allowed him to have affairs?" Donnell asked, understanding many couples agreed to an open marriage.

"Yes, as long as he was discreet about it." Brandy confirmed.

"Was this before or after you were born?"

"Before. But her plan backfired."

"Your sister?" Donnell asked.

"Her mother." Brandy replied, finishing the content in her glass. "My mom never planned on my dad falling in love with another woman. But he had, and when he told her, she didn't want the embarrassment of a divorce, so she suggested they try to reconcile. That's how I was conceived. The trial period between reconciling. It didn't work, and my mother left my father unaware she was pregnant with me. That's why me and my sister are so close in age. It was almost two months after my mother left that she realized she was pregnant. She wasn't going to be pregnant and divorced. She agreed to keep up pretenses, and my father could still have the woman he loved." Brandy finished, and Donnell could see the perplexity on her face.

"Here, you need this more than me." he said, handing her his wine glass. She took it without a second glance and drank.

"What were they thinking?" she said, not actually asking him but more so speaking her thoughts out loud.

"I don't know." Donnell honestly didn't have an answer for her. The dynamic was messy, but for whatever reason all three parties agreed to the arrangement. He couldn't imagine that type of situation, but to each their own. He wanted to focus on them, if there could still be a them.

"I don't want secrets between us, Donnell." Her voice was slightly sterner than when she'd spoken before.

"I don't want to keep secrets from you, Brandy. But I can't promise you that when it comes to my cases."

"I know, and I'm not asking for that. I just felt so stupid when that FBI agent told me you were involved, that you set me up and knew about the investment company's fraudulent funds. He even said you were the one to give the intel to the FBI."

"That part is actually true. I knew they were involved in a few joint ventures in the US. I hadn't investigated beyond that or discovered how the money was being used. That's the difference between the CIA and the FBI. The FBI handles transactions conducted on American soil. I handle things outside of it."

"But that's just it. If I had known at least that bit of information, I wouldn't have had any reason to believe any of it. I was completely blindsided."

"I know, and I'm sorry, I won't let anything like this ever happen again."

"I hope not. I only plan to be arrested once in my lifetime." She teased.

He laughed while standing up, taking the glass from her hand, and placing it on the small table. Donnell helped Brandy to stand. Pulling her into his arms, he felt hope and pride, as she willingly put her arms around his back, and looked up at him.

"I won't let something like that happen again, believe me. And outside of the CIA, I won't keep anything else from you, I promise." he said.

"I'm going to hold you to that, Donnell Mason." she said, arching her neck to allow her lips to meet his in a kiss. He pressed his lips against hers urgently, probing her mouth to open with his tongue, and when she allowed him access, he mated his mouth to hers. Donnell missed the feeling of having her in his arms and making love to her mouth. A couple jogging by the pond whistled, interrupting their kiss. The couple waved, and Brandy waved back.

"Do you know them?" Donnell asked.

"Yes, they live a couple of apartments over. I think it is so sweet how they go jogging together." Brandy admitted.

"We could go jogging around the pond if you want." he suggested.

"You'd be into doing that?" she asked.

"Baby, I'm into doing anything with you."

"Is that so?" she questioned, quickly giving him a chaste kiss.

"Of course."

"How about feeding me?"

"Absolutely."

"Making love to me?"

"Definitely."

"Then we should order some food because we have some making up to do."

"Oh really?" he asked, feeling her rotate her hips against him slowly.

"Uh-hmm." she cooed as he tried to stifle the groan escaping his mouth.

"You're playing with fire, Brandy." he warned.

"No, actually, I'm starting the fire." She said, leaning up to kiss him again.

"We'll order the food later." he said, reaching for the balcony door and practically dragging her inside. She laughed and instantly ran for the bedroom as he closed the door. "Don't run from me now, woman." he said, running after her.

Brandy laid next to Donnell, both her stomach and body satisfied. They made love twice, once before the food arrived and once afterward. She couldn't help the grin on her face. She looked over at Donnell, who was lying completely still with a delighted smile on his face.

"Donnie." she called.

"Yes."

"Since we're being honest with no secrets, I have a question to ask you." He opened his eyes and turned his head to look at her.

"Ask me anything you want." he responded.

"Does Dustin Shaw own Shaw Realty Group?"

"Yes, among other things." he answered.

"Did you ask him to buy the strip mall the bakery is leased out of?" she asked and watched as Donnell belted out a laugh before looking back at her.

"No, but I'm not surprised if he did." he said, then continued to explain his conversation with Dustin and Dominic helping the patrons who also received fraudulent funds from the investment company.

"Wait, so BCF is Dominic Blake's company?" she asked, and Donnell nodded. She lay there in awe. Blake Capital Funding, she discovered, had refinanced her loan and purchased all of her equipment under the same terms. Donnell's friends not only helped her, but the other small business owners, with capital funding, and lease financing.

"I can't believe you did that for me." she admitted. He shifted from his back onto his side and faced her.

"Brandy, I would do anything for you." he said. She sighed inwardly, then leaned over and kissed him. No one had ever done something like that for her before.

"Thank you." she said sincerely after ending their kiss.

"You're welcome." he replied. They stared at one another for a minute before a thought popped into her mind.

"Hey, we need to discuss something else?" Brandy said.

"What is it?"

"We haven't talked about my feelings towards marriage." She began, noting the recognition in his eyes of the conversation at Blake Manor a few weeks back.

"No, we haven't." he replied.

"Is that a deal-breaker for you?" she asked nervously. Most guys she dated would love the thought of never having to worry about getting married. But Brandy knew Donnell was different. His parents were still happily married after forty years. Brandy watched as his eyes left hers and shifted to the ceiling as he thought on her question.

"It's not." He admitted, looking back over at her.

"Are you sure? I know you like traditions." She questioned. Donnell was unlike any man she'd ever met. She knew that the moment he'd told her about helping prep Thanksgiving dinner at his grandmother's house.

"I do like traditions, but I'm not bound by them. I understand your reservations and unfavorable views on marriage. Not every couple that loves each other gets married, just like, not every couple that gets married loves each other."

"Is that your way of telling me you love me?" she teased. Donnell closed his eyes and chuckled before meeting her eyes again.

"Is that your way of asking me if I love you?"

"Maybe?" she answered with a mild shrug. His eyes grew more intense as the silence lingered around them.

Donnell slowly lifted his hand to her chin, then traced her bottom lip with his thumb. She shuttered inwardly at his touch.

"Yes, Brandy. I do love you." He admitted. Brandy couldn't stop the smile forming on her face if she wanted to. She pushed her lips against his thumb before leaning over to kiss his lips. Donnell gladly accepted her kiss.

"I love you too." She said, ending their kiss and resting her forehead against his.

"I'm glad to hear it." Donnell said, resting on his back and gathering her in his arms. They lay in silence before another thought popped into Brandy's mind.

"So, you've met my parents. Does this mean I get to meet yours?" she asked.

"Maybe, I might be persuaded." he teased.

"Is that so? Do you think I'm not up for the challenge?" she teased back.

"Do your worst." he challenged.

"Stay right here." she said, and laughed at his slight frown as she shifted out of his arms to leave the bed.

"Hey, where are you going?" he mildly protested.

"I'll be right back." she said, moving so he couldn't grab her and bring her back into the bed. She had a special surprise for him. Running to the kitchen, she grabbed the container of the special treats she'd made for him. Brandy had planned to mail them to him if he hadn't spoken to her at the party. Her grandmother told her the way to a man's heart was his stomach, but it was satisfying Donnell's sweet tooth in her case. Tossing them in the microwave for ten seconds, she yelled.

"Close your eyes."

"They're closed," he called back. "But not seeing doesn't affect my hearing or my smell." She rolled her eyes as the microwave dinged and grabbed the treats to put them on a plate.

"Ready or not, here I come. Are your eyes still closed?" Brandy asked, walking back into her bedroom.

"Yes." he replied.

"Okay. Sit up just a little and rest your back against the headboard." Donnell did as she asked.

"Keep your eyes closed."

"Brandy, I am not going to open my eyes, but whatever you have smells fantastic."

"Wait until you taste it?" she said, climbing up on the bed.

"I could say the same things about you." he teased.

"Lie still. I'm going to straddle you." she said while balancing the little plate in her hand.

"You will find no complaints with that request." He answered with a grin.

"Is that so?" she said, settling herself just above his groin.

"I'm completely at your mercy."

"Okay, now open your mouth." She watched as he did as she instructed and took the treat from the plate and gently placed it at the tip of his mouth. He instinctively bit down, and she watched him sample the delicacy.

"Good lord, what was that?" he asked, opening both his eyes and mouth to devour the rest of it.

"A very unique brownie."

"That tasted better than any brownie I've ever had."

"I found this recipe on a website called Sultry Treats. I thought you would like it."

"Baby, I loved it." he admitted, sitting up further, reaching out to balance her on his lap and allowing her to feed him another one.

"So, have I convinced you enough to meet your parents?"

"After that, you can meet my entire family." he said, licking his lips. She chuckled, then leaned forward to lick a tiny speck of chocolate from the corner of his mouth.

"I guess from now on, when I want to bribe you, I'll have to break out my sultry treat recipe." she teased. Donnell smiled, took the plate from her hand and placed it on the nightstand. Then surprised her by flipping her on her back.

"You won't ever have to bribe me, but right now, I'm gonna make you my sultry treat." he said.

"You'll find no complaints here." she replied, placing her arms around his neck and bringing his lips to hers.

Epilogue

"Good evening, Mr. Storm." Marvin said, opening the door to Blake Manor as Damien stepped into the foyer. "Mr. and Mrs. Blake are out at the moment."

"That's fine, Marvin. I'm actually here to check on Ms. Walden."

"Yes, sir. She's been out on the property for a while today." Damien nodded. "Shall I get you anything?" Marvin offered.

"No, Marvin, but thank you." Damien strolled through the foyer, passing by the kitchen, through the sitting room, and out to the deck. Trekking down the stairs onto the cobblestone walkway, he took the path to the left toward the four-bedroom colonial that sat behind Blake Manor. Why he continued to do this every year, he didn't understand. Well, that wasn't entirely true. He did it because no one else did, and besides the tough exterior she put on every year, today was the one day she needed someone, or at least that's what he convinced himself.

Noticing the feeling of the cobblestone turning into pavement, he passed by the side of the house and the childhood playset he'd spent many afternoons on as a child. The secluded area on the Blake Estate came into view. The only access for entry behind the house and the resting place of the two prior generations of the Blake family. As the pavement turned to grass, he caught sight of her. She was sitting in front of her parents' tombstones on the quilted blanket given to her by her mother on her fourth birthday. Never knowing a few months later it would be the last gift she'd ever received. He placed his hands in his pockets and slowly walked over to her. She didn't turn her head to acknowledge his presence, didn't look over as he sat on the edge of the blanket beside her. Damien brought his knees up as he sat, resting his forearm on them, and looked straight ahead. She didn't speak, and neither did he. Damien decided a long time ago to always be there for her, and though in every other aspect of her life she seemed to need no one, now was the one time she didn't refute.

Doing as he did every year, Damien read the name on the tombstone of his godparents, Richard and Andrea Walden. To the left, another set of tombstones of two people he considered his surrogate grandparents, Donald and Elaine Blake, and further down another set etched with the names Andrew and Catherine Blake. These men and women were as much a part of his life as they had been their own children and grandchildren. He finally glanced over at Shannon, noticing the tears that were dried on her face. He placed his arm around her to comfort her. The only time he could, without her rejecting him. She leaned into him, nestled her head on his shoulder. The afternoon breeze flowed over them as he continued to hold her. And then he felt her shift, and not in a way he'd ever felt before. He looked down, and his eyes connected to her light brown ones. The dimples in her cheeks were evident without a smile. She looked at him in a way he'd never seen before. Longing, or maybe desire reflected in them. Damien blinked twice, clearly needing his head examined, completely feeling like a jerk in the way his mind was playing tricks on him. He started to pull away until he saw her eyes slowly avert to his lips and then back up to his eyes. His breath caught in his throat, and he swallowed hard. The beating of his heart began to increase. He knew that look, having seen it a thousand times, from plenty of women, but never from her. Never from her. He was stuck on what to make of it. Did he want to kiss her? Of course, he did. Was she in the most vulnerable state? Of course, she was. Would Dominic kill him if he ever found out? Probably. Stuck. That's what he was. For the first time in his life, he didn't know what choice to make. This wasn't some random girl or groupie.

This was Shannon, his best friend's cousin, his mother's best friend's daughter, the one woman entirely off-limits to him. But how could he deny what he was feeling? How long could he keep fighting the temptation right in front of him? Feeling her in his arms, the longing in her eyes, the fullness of her lips.

True to form, she took the decision out of his hands, tilting her lips toward his, and he met her halfway. An electrical force shot through him the moment their lips touched, causing him almost to lose his balance. She let out a soft moan that nearly undid him. He brought her further into his arms, melting his tongue to hers and devouring every inch of her mouth. Damien knew he was crossing the line into prohibited territory, drifting into impermissible waters, sinking into the sweetest taboo as he savored every taste of the one thing forbidden to him.

Bonus Scene: After Arion's Party.

Anita Campbell allowed Dustin to assist her in taking a seat in the Blake family living room. Dominic and Ashiree's friends were in the sitting room, continuing to talk after the birthday party was over. Anita had watched from a distance, fighting the longing to embrace the extension of her family that she now knew existed. She had a daughter, a son-in-law and a grandson. The last couple of years, she'd felt like a surrogate mother to Dustin and a few of the hands on his ranch. Also, to Tricia, Dustin's wife since they'd reunited.

Anita watched as her daughter sat on the sofa next to hers. Ashiree smiled lovingly at her husband, who stood behind her with his hand on her shoulder. Finally, looking over at her, she smiled.

"How did you enjoy the party, Ms. Anita? I'm sure it was a little strange since it was for a one-year-old." Ashiree asked.

"I enjoyed it quite well. He is quite the little man." Anita praised.

"Thank you. I'm so happy you could come. Tricia has been telling me how Dustin keeps you trapped on his farm." Ashiree said teasingly.

"I actually love being on the farm. It is a far cry from city life."

"Yes, it is." Ashiree agreed.

"I'm also looking into moving closer to Houston. Dustin agreed to help me." Anita informed.

"Oh?" Ashiree inquired. Anita glanced over at Dustin, who gave her an encouraging nod.

"Yes. I've recently discovered my daughter lives here."

"Have you?" Ashiree replied with a smile.

"Yes, thanks to your friend Donnell."

"Oh, Donnie's great, isn't he?" Ashiree stated and Anita heard a partial groan come from Dominic. She noticed Ashiree look over her shoulder at him with a playful smile.

"He is, and quite tall." Anita added.

"That he is. He helped me find my brother. I'm so grateful to him for that." Ashiree admitted.

"I've heard. Congratulations."

"Thank you. It's not perfect, but I'm hopeful." Ashiree said.

"I feel the same about meeting my daughter."

"Meeting her? You haven't met her?" Ashiree asked.

"No, unfortunately, I gave her up for adoption because of my illness."

"I'm sure that was hard. I can't imagine it, especially now that I have Arion. Did a good family adopt her?"

"I believed so. I did not get the chance to meet the couple, but I heard wonderful things about them." Anita replied.

"Do you know how her life is now? Is she doing well?"

"I believe she is doing very well. She has a family of her own now." Anita said, doing her best not to look over at Dominic. Her hands were in her lap and slightly moist.

"Have you talked to her yet?" Ashiree asked.

"No, and I'm afraid I won't say the right words. A lot of time has passed. I had so many moments when I didn't think I'd survive and my efforts to find her before were unsuccessful." Anita replied.

"I don't think there are any perfect words Ms. Anita. But I can guess she's probably wondering or wondered why you had to give her up. I would suggest just telling her the truth. It isn't always pretty, and it may not get the result you want, but it's better than being left in the dark." Anita's heart ached, listening to the sorrow in Ashiree's voice. She knew it was partially due to her absence, but she was sure Ashiree was referring to the outcome of finding her father. Tricia explained to Anita the reunion had not gone as planned, and Ashiree had yet to meet her father. She was at a loss for words. How did she tell her who she was? How did she assure her that if given a chance, she would gladly be in her life?

"They say practice makes perfect." Dominic said from behind Ashiree. Anita met his gaze, and he nodded encouragingly to help her continue.

"I think that's a good idea." Dustin further encouraged. "What do you think, Ashiree?" Dustin continued. Ashiree looked over at Dustin with a puzzled look, then over her shoulder to Dominic, before looking back at her.

"Sure." She shrugged. "I can play stand-in." Ashiree agreed. Anita took a deep breath and glanced back over to Dustin. Her nerves were in a jumbled mess and her hands were partially shaking.

"Go on, Ms. Anita." Dustin urged. "If Ashiree, were your daughter, what would you say to her?" Anita looked back over to her Ashiree, who displayed a helpful smile. Anita's eyes began to water with tears.

"That I planned to find her. I never wanted to give her up. I thought I had time. I didn't mean for things to turn out the way they did." She admitted sorrowfully as tears slowly began to fall from her eyes.

"How did you plan to find her?" Dustin continued to push. She did a quick look over to Dustin then back at Ashiree. She was still smiling and nodding for her to continue.

"I named her." She said, tears flowing more freely than before. "Something that was uncommon, something I could easily find."

"What happened?" Ashiree asked, reaching over to grab Anita's hand in support. She gripped it tightly, finally touching her daughter.

"I don't know." She admitted.

"What about the adoptive parents?" Anita heard Dominic ask. She closed her eyes, trying to fight the years of hurt and anguish she'd put them both through.

"It's okay, you're doing good." She heard Ashiree say. Anita opened her eyes to stare back at her. Knowing Ashiree would finally understand when she answered Dominic's question. Her hands began to tremble lightly.

"They died on the way to the hospital to pick her up." Anita watched the encouraging smile on Ashiree's face slowly morph from confusion to slight unbelief.

"What did you name her?" Dustin asked.

"Aushrey, after my mother, Audrey, and her father, Austin." Anita answered, looking at Ashiree as her eyes slowly welled up in tears and her bottom lip began to shudder. Anita had no idea what she was thinking and dreaded the thought of her letting go of her trembling hand. Anita watched with bated breath as Ashiree looked over at her husband, who nodded yes to her silent question. An audible cry escaped her lips as she slowly leaned forward and fell to her knees in front of Anita. Anita cupped her face as tears flowed freely from both their eyes.

"I need to hear you say it." Ashiree pleaded in a croaked voice. Anita brought her face closer to Ashiree.

"I'm your mother." she admitted. Ashiree laid in her lap and silently wailed. Anita comforted her daughter, embraced her, stroked her hair, and kissed her forehead, for the first time.

About the Author

MzSassytheAuthor is a mother of three from Detroit, MI and resides in Texas. Her love for reading started in her childhood years with book series like "The Babysitters' Club". Most of her adolescent years were spent writing poetry, but it wasn't until her adult years that she discovered her love for writing; particularly connecting stories and reoccurring characters. She loves family and friend relationships and displays them in her writing. She enjoys traveling, attending sporting events, puzzles and of course snuggling up to read a good book.

Thanks for reading! Please add a short review on Amazon or Goodreads and let us know what you thought!

Made in the USA
Monee, IL
07 December 2023

48312136R00152